UNTHANK

An anthology of short stories from the MA in Creative Writing at the University of East Anglia

We would like to thank the following for their help and advice:
Eastern Arts Association
Jon Cook
Andy Vargo and Mike Oakes of the Norfolk Institute of Art and Design
Lucy Clibbon
Dominic Belisario

The publishers wish to thank Warner Chappell Music Ltd for permission to re-produce the lyrics from "Thin line between love and hate" on pages 123-124

ISBN 0 9515009 0 2

Published by the Centre for Creative and Performing Arts,
University of East Anglia, Norwich.

Printed and bound by Richard Clay Ltd of Bungay, Suffolk.

Set in Linotype Sabon, 11/13.

Contents

Malcolm Bradbury

INTRODUCTION

S ometime in 1970, Angus Wilson and I - two writing
Professors in the School of English and American
Studies at the University of East Anglia - began talking
about whether it was possible to establish a serious
course in creative writing in a British university. Creative writing was, more or less, a non-existent subject in the British
groves of academe. It seemed largely an American invention,
and in fact both of us had participated in several programmes
in the USA, some of them very good, some less impressive. I
had been in a programme at Indiana that had taught me a
good deal, and perhaps most importantly, thrown me together
with a group of other writers whose ideas and innovations had
sharpened my own professional senses enormously. I discovered that there were many skills in writing that could be
shared and learned, that it was important to live in a world
inhabited by other literary contemporaries, and that writing
was vastly more important than innocent inspiration.

In Britain at the beginning of the 1970s things did not look entirely promising. Serious fiction was having a hard time, as publishing houses turned into conglomerates and increasingly aimed at mass markets. There was a shortage of good literary magazines, following a spate of periodical deaths in the 1950s and 1960s. The short story in Britain seemed something of a dying form. Criticism had little to do with creation, and vice versa; and so the gap between practising writers and the academy was, if anything, widening, with a fair amount of condescension on both sides. Meanwhile critical theory was growing more abstract and theoretical, and moving attention away from the creative process, the author, the imaginative text or the great literary ideas toward the lexical sign, reception theory, the theory of literary production, and the notion of the Death of the Author. If it seemed important to try to reconcile the two, not only for the good of creation but for the good of criticism, it also seemed a difficult moment to do it.

So these were the weighty matters in our minds as we explored the idea of a serious, professionally orientated creative writing course with our colleagues and the university - a university that had, happily, committed itself more than most to the study of contemporary literature and had boldly appointed onto its faculty, writer-critics like ourselves. It is the fate of authors like ourselves to receive a good many unpublished as well as unexpected and unsolicited manuscripts through the post, and we both knew that there were a good number of young unpublished writers of real merit. Some of these, we felt (not all, for not everyone works best in the open), might benefit from the right kind of course - a detailed, intensive workshop that allowed writing-in-progress to be examined in detail, in a critical atmosphere, over the period of a year. The writers existed, but the courses didn't, and we planned a workshop course in fiction, based on sustained writing that would also link up with the other intellectual and critical activities of a busy graduate programme largely concerned with modern fiction.

As we talked, good fortune befell us. We were telephoned by a recent Sussex graduate who had heard rumour of these plans, and was interested in this kind of a course. His name was Ian McEwan, and the work he submitted impressed us both so much that we began the programme a year earlier than we had planned. Ian was the only student, and we were finding our way. Over that year Ian wrote something like 30 short stories, and had the basis of his first and second books. We pointed his work toward American magazines, and he duly appeared in *Transatlantic Review* and the *New American Review*. In 1975, after the usual struggles, his first collection of short stories *First Love, Last Rites* appeared from Jonathan Cape, and a notable career began. By this time other remarkable writers were starting to come through the now-developing programme. Clive Sinclair had written his first novel, called *Bibliosexuality*, while a UEA undergraduate - so, incidentally, had another UEA graduate, Rose Tremain - and when he returned to do a Ph.D. in American literature, he joined in the course. Kazuo Ishiguro and a fine American writer, Jodie K. Klavans, also came into the programme and both were soon published. When we lost Angus Wilson by retirement, Angela Carter came on to the teaching team, and when her life became too busy Rose Tremain came back to join in the teaching.

If the Creative Writing MA has a single purpose, it is to encourage the production of serious fiction, but many different kinds of writer have come into it. Over recent years important writers as various as Dierdre Madden (*The Birds of the Innocent Wood*), Glenn Patterson (*Burning Your Own*) and Mark Illis (*A Chinese Summer*) have been members. There have been new writers who have not yet seen print, and writers already well-published. There have been British writers, and Irish, American, Italian and Jordanian writers. There have been recent graduates and professional people of eminent mien and more mature years, like David Rose of ITN, who will surely not mind the description. There have been traditionalists and avant gardeists, epic sweepers and miniaturists. There have been Postmodernists and Postfeminists, and people who scorn all titles. The record of successful publication has been high and the recent publishing season has seen a burst of output from recent and not so recent graduates, including Mark Illis, Ann Enright, Kathy Page, Stephen Hargrave, Paul Stewart and James Sorel-Cameron. There have been Whitbread Prizes (McEwan, Ishiguro), Betty Trask Prizes (Patterson), the Rooney Prize (Dierdre Madden) and a good many writing fellowships.

As for the programme itself, it has over time multiplied in several directions, helped by various publishers and agents who have taken an interest in it. There is a related Eastern Arts Association Fellowship which has been held by many splendid fellows, including Alan Burns, Wilson Harris, Anthony Thwaite, Snoo Wilson, Adam Mars-Jones, David Lodge, Maggie Gee, Paul Muldoon, Fleur Adcock and George Macbeth, who have contributed greatly to the meeting, the teaching, and the writing. There is now a strong undergraduate programme (we deliberately began with a professionally-intentioned course for writers in whom we had great confidence), which includes fiction, poetry, playwriting and filmscript writing. There is a publishing course in collaboration with the Norfolk Institute of Art and Design. Now to develop all these elements and to extend our links with the world of publishing, drama, television and film, there is a new Centre of Creative and Performing Arts in the School, directed by Jon Cook. And there is also our first Ph.D. student in Creative Writing, the Jordanian novelist Fadir Faqir, author of *Nisanit*.

There is also this anthology, the first but I hope not the last. It comes from the students in a single - and, I may say, exceptional - year (1988-89). Four of the students, Gerri Brightwell, Caroline Forbes, Saul Hyman and Mark Slater came up with the idea of the anthology and followed it through from typewriter to typesetter, as a project for the publishing course run in conjunction with the Norfolk Institute of Art and Design. This involved a great deal of effort, designing page lay-outs, collating and correcting copy and arranging funding. Their anthology, representative of the writing at a certain point in the course, shows the range as well as the quality of the work produced. It can be left to the reader to decide whether there are common qualities that link these writers together. The common ground I see is some strong ideas about the nature and prospects of serious fiction, together with a self-demanding professional quality, the stuff a writer needs. These are, I think and I hope, writers you have not heard the last of. As one of them - Alan Wilkinson - has said, it can be a burden as well as an opportunity to come into a course that now actually has a history, and the pressure is on. But I think you will find that the writers here have risen to it.

Gerri Brightwell

THE FISH CORPSE

There was a small explosion in his rice as the fish landed. It lay open-mouthed on his plate, its short copper body quite still except for a slight trembling at the gills. John stared at it for a moment then, tracing an imagined path, raised his eyes to the sky straight above. A bird was circling high over the patio: a gull, he supposed, they went for fish.

He cupped one hand above his eyes and watched as the bird floated towards the hills on the other side of the bay. There were no sunshades over the tables and his face was beginning to scorch. In a few seconds the bird had dissolved in the haze where the tops of the hills melted into the the sky. He hadn't expected Cannes to be so hot, it was only May. But then it didn't seem like Cannes, not with the sun shining such a fierce white, not with this clutter of small china bowls on the table, each with its own china spoon.

His head was throbbing. His first trip abroad with the company and he felt dull from the heat. He looked across at Tomlinson sitting opposite. A quick smile. To his right sat the

French girl - he searched for her name: Gabrielle, he thought, something like that. She had her back to him, taking a bowl of rice from one of her colleagues and trying to find a space for it on the table. He scanned the other six faces: no-one had seen. There was another bowl of rice right in front of him. He took up the spoon and piled on enough to cover the fish, then dropped the spoon back into the bowl and ran a hand through his hair. His hair was so hot it burnt his fingers, smooth to the touch and damp at the roots from his sweat. He leant onto his elbows, the weight of his head in his hands, and stared down at his plate. The piled rice lay quite still. Too much rice: a give-away like uneven earth over a murdered body.

It had happened so quickly he hadn't had time to think. That was his problem - he could hear Mr James saying it - he didn't think. He looked down the table to where Mr James was sitting, leaning back in his chair in his shirt sleeves. He was talking to Gabrielle's boss, a cigarette held lazily between two fingers, carving figures in the air with his hands. Every now and again a shrug of the shoulders, slightly French. Mr James would have summoned a waiter, requested a fresh plate and more rice. No confusion, no fuss. But then Mr James wasn't a man into whose plate a fish would have fallen from the sky.

The only waiter on the terrace was across the other side busy clearing a table. John tried a few phrases in his mind...*Ce poisson* - he couldn't think of the word for to fall, he would have to mime that - fell...*du ciel*. Was that right? *This fish fell from the sky.* He could imagine the blank look on the Chinese waiter's face. He would have to give him the plate and point at the fish. If the waiter spoke to him he would be lost. The waiter had said something to him as he sat down: very clipped French, he hadn't caught a single word. But at that moment Mr James had called him over to his end of the table and, with barely a glance at the menu, ordered food for the whole party.

The waiter disappeared into the shadows. Anyway, John had

buried the fish, he would have had to dig it out of the rice. One of the others might have seen him doing it. Besides, the grains were gluey, they would probably have stuck to the fish and left marks of starch to cloud the scales: obviously not a freshly fallen fish but one that had been lying in rice for some minutes. How could a goldfish have got into the rice? The restaurant staff would have been suspicious, surely. And it was Mr James who had chosen this place, he came here every year. He knew the owner.

John shifted his chair back to give himself room to take off his jacket, and hung it over the back of his chair. His armpits were prickling with sweat and his shirt clung to his skin. He should have taken it off when they arrived, but he'd hesitated and thought it best not to. His face was flushed, he could feel it throbbing as it burned in the noon sun. With the back of his hand he wiped the sweat from his top lip, noticing as he did the dark marks on his shirt where it ran under his arms. Trickles slid down his back, making him shiver despite the heat. Tomlinson was still in his jacket, with only a slight sheen of sweat on his face. His balding scalp shone damply as he nodded, putting questions to the man on his right in slow English while he picked at a piece of bread. Tomlinson had come last year, and the year before.

Gabrielle still had her back to him, talking away, or arguing. He looked down at his plate. Possibly the fish was still alive. He wondered. Maybe he should just have picked it up and put it in the ashtray. His mind reeled back to when the fish had lain naked on the rice. He could have reached out, taken it by the tail and dropped it into the ashtray. Now it lay under the rice. Dead. He decided it was dead. Immediately the rice looked heavy, tainted. Inedible.

Tomlinson let out a chuckle. John's head jerked up only to see Tomlinson nodding as he laughed, nodding slowly, very slowly, with his eyes on John's plate.

"And her husband never found out?" he asked, turning back.

"Never. A very clever woman," and the Frenchman tapped the side of his head. They both laughed.

The base of John's throat was pulsing uncomfortably. His chest felt tight. He tried to breathe deeply as he stared out past Tomlinson at the bay. A yacht leaned far into the white of its sail and silently disappeared, at what must have been a tearing speed, behind Tomlinson's shoulder. Up here there was no breeze at all, leaving the air to hang heavily like liquid glass. He dug his fingers into his collar and tugged, squinting. The sun glaring off the ocean stung his eyes. His sunglasses were at home, in England. Too casual, he'd decided. But here they all wore them, all the French. He shielded his eyes with his hand for a moment, then closed them.

"Come on, lad." Tomlinson was smiling across at him. "Come on," and he passed him a dish. "That's the beef in spicy black bean sauce." John took the dish and smiled back. The rice waited on his plate. The dish was hot, only the edges cool enough to hold. The rich smell of the meat rose up to fill his nostrils as he spooned a little onto his plate, away from the rice. The sauce ran, staining some of the rice brown. His fingers were straining under the weight of the dish so he shifted his grip slightly to load up the spoon again. He emptied it next to the rice, then took more before passing the dish to Gabrielle.

Tomlinson was already holding out another to him. "Chicken with cashew nuts." John smiled again and took it. He piled a low mound next to the beef and passed it on to Gabrielle with a fainter smile. The plates were small. His already looked full, three mounds: beef, chicken. And the rice.

"Prawns and something. You'll like that, you go for seafood, don't you lad?" and the dish was pushed at him. John opened his mouth to say no. "Go on then, take it will you," and he took it. He took the spoon and scraped it across the bottom of the metal dish, filling it with prawns in an over-red sauce.

There was only one space left: he dumped the prawns straight on top of the rice, and heaped on more, then more. He could just have passed the dish on, he knew that, and he watched the sauce colouring the rice red. Blood, he thought. He took up his fork and stabbed a prawn onto its prongs.

"Bon appetit." Gabrielle was smiling at him. "Oh - you haven't a drink," and she reached for a bottle. The wine poured noisily into his glass. Hers was half-empty but she still raised it: "Santé," so John put down his fork and picked up his glass by the stem.

"Santé," he replied and took a sip. The wine was red and sucked at the juices of his mouth. Blood red, he thought. He took a mouthful and put it down. Where it was empty the sun showed up his fingermarks, his greasy fingermarks that clouded the glass. He imagined the fish in its bed of rice: clouded fishscales, sticky with starch. It was obscene, a goldfish in his rice, a raw goldfish. The bird must have taken it from a pond, easy prey, then dropped it. An ornamental fish, inedible. Not like tuna or mackerel, herring, cod or plaice; fish meant as food.

The top of his head was pounding under the sun. He could feel his thoughts coming slowly, singly, as if the heat was separating them out. He reached for his fork with its speared prawn. The congealing sauce stuck to it, a thick red; he examined it closely. He closed his eyes, put it into his mouth, and chewed. It didn't taste like anything he'd ever eaten in a Chinese restaurant before. It was all wrong. This place was all wrong with its forks and plates, baskets of bread and bottles of red wine.

His eyes open, he carried on chewing, the pieces going round and round in his mouth like bits of polystyrene. He tried to swallow but couldn't, and instead stared into his plate, at the prawns, at the rice. The sauce must have soaked right through by now, down to the fish, the dead fish. The sauce had a funny taste to it. He couldn't eat any more. He reached for his wine to wash down what was in his mouth, and just as the glass came level with his lips he brought it down heavily onto the table. Shoving his chair back he made off across the terrace, one hand clamped over his mouth to hold in the dead prawn.

Barbara Cocks

THE BLACK CAT

lizabeth crept downstairs clutching her dressing gown at the neck. She thought the faint rings on James's tummy might not have been there the night before. Or they could have been there for a week? She would never have noticed if she hadn't insisted on bathing him herself.

Like a fugitive in her own house she pushed the study door and slipped inside. It was the warmest room in the house, the only place she could collect her thoughts. Sometimes she'd sit there for hours. She enjoyed being surrounded by books even when she was only sitting and drinking coffee. Her books gave her a sense of belonging. Milton's business associates brought them for her, now and then. Otherwise they came to her through the post.

Well her books weren't much use to her now. Sitting at the edge of her chair, a fist drummed into her cheek, she thought, she didn't want anyone to come near her, not until she'd sorted things out. Should she take him to the doctor or would she wait and see what happened? Probably it was just an allergy. Something he'd eaten or the soap. At home she wouldn't have hesitated but, here, everything was different. People went to the doctor only as a last resort.

But wasn't she being silly? It wasn't as if she were one of them. People like her were so much more protected. For a start they were better off. And the house, even though they were renting it, was her home.

Looking up, she noticed the room was just as she'd left it the night before. The magazines were stacked, open, on the coffee-table. The ash-tray was overflowing. The embers were still in the grate. The whisky bottle was empty. The medical encyclopedia had the pages marked. She liked books and papers piled up, somewhere she didn't have to fuss, but then, what was the point of having servants?

Matilde wouldn't lift a finger, not in here, Elizabeth thought. Not unless you stood over her. Then she pouted and worked slowly, lifting her arms as if they had lead weights attached. Two years ago she had been persuaded to take the books down from the shelves but that had only happened once. Once in two years.

Elizabeth imagined the dust and thought, what did it matter, her books weren't her friends anymore, not the way they used to be. She needed them to help her forget her whereabouts. It hadn't always been like that. She hadn't always considered herself as just the wife of the overseas engineer. What she needed was the courage to make her own decisions.

After all they were only the faintest of marks. You could barely see them. Probably, by evening, they'd have disappeared. It wasn't chicken pox or measles. He'd been through all that. What if she were to call the doctor? He'd probably be more than sympathetic. Supposing Matilde found out – what did it matter to her what anyone, here, thought? They could do what they liked. The company would pay.

As for Milton – what was the point of asking him? You handle it, he'd say. Take him to the doctor if you're worried.

Oh, and don't forget, we're invited this evening. And if she burst into tears, and said it was all just too much, he'd say what she needed was to get a hold on herself and get down to the business of learning the language. Or, he'd blame it on the altitude, Elizabeth thought. Funnily enough, she hadn't noticed the altitude much. Maybe because they'd come up slowly. Mexico, Cuzco, then La Paz.

Out there, beyond the trees, beyond the garden she loved, were the peaks of the great snow-capped mountains, Illimani and Illampu. It had taken her sometime to get the names right. At the foot of Illimani was a skiing resort. They'd go there sometime. Milton and James would love it. As for her, she didn't ski but she enjoyed walking about. Once she'd asked Matilde about walking in the mountains. Matilde looked away and muttered that no-one went there.

"Yes they do," Elizabeth contradicted her, thinking of the Prudencios, Milton's rich Bolivian business partners.

"You mustn't go," Matilde said, and mumbled something about the mountains being haunted by the Khariciri. The Khariciri was an evil spirit, conceived of, at one time, as a wandering figure in black, a priest, maybe, at the time of the Conquest, then, later, as any foreigner found wandering about. He, or she, was thought to have the power to enter a hut, unknown to the inhabitants, and melt the fat off babies.

Elizabeth couldn't see what the Khariciri had to do with them. They were here because Milton was building a road that would link Bolivia to the Pacific, a road that could be used for getting goods to market, replacing the tortuous routes that twisted around the mountains, then, she thought, Matilde was warning her of something else, a landslide, perhaps?

"You musn't go," Matilde insisted and when Elizabeth asked, "Why ever not?" Matilde had shaken her heavy plaits and said the mountain paths were sacred and a foreigner had no way of knowing where he was treading.

So much for that. Elizabeth stood up as if she'd reached a decision. Crossing the room she drew the curtains and flung the windows wide. The air was still cold despite the intensity of the sunlight. It was so strange, here, the way the ultra-violet light could burn your skin and yet the cold air hurt your lungs if you were to breathe too sharply or deeply. The temperature varied, immensely, from sun to shade. The drop could be as dramatic as fifteen or twenty degrees. What to wear was always a problem.

Elizabeth was thinking about her clothes, and about how the fine alpaca vests she'd brought went well with her silk shirts from Canada, when something flashed at the periphery of her vision. At first she thought it might have been a picaflor darting from the mulberry trees to the red-hot pokers, there and back, a whirr of emerald and gold, and, for once, the Spanish word came readily into her head. Perhaps she was becoming acclimatized? Then, with a start, she realized that what she'd seen was the predatory movement of the cat.

The cat was a coal black, fluffy, bundle of tricks. They'd kept it for James's sake. He spent half his day with the cat, as did Matilde, who fed it and stroked it and sat with it curled up on her lap, most of the afternoon, or whenever she was taking a break, outside, sitting and rocking in her chair. Probably she was out there now.

Elizabeth caught him staring at her, his wide eyes looking at her. He straightened his back and brought his face up to the level of the window. "Oh!" she said, alarmed. "I didn't know you were there."

But she had known, intuitively, just as she knew that, on the other side of the valley, beyond the dun-coloured stretch of river, a string of diminutive figures were scrambling up and down the face of the cliff. Why were they always carrying things, Elizabeth wondered?

Matilde had told her that when the river dried up whole

families moved to shelter beneath the bridge, outcasts who fed off the refuse the garbage women dumped on the floor of the valley. She couldn't see anyone there from where she was standing. She could only see the tops of the trees and the gate, at the end of their driveway, but she knew that, on the other side of the valley, there was a massively-eroded landscape, with craters and columns of mud, and a river-bed that was sometimes dried up, sometimes in flood.

"Mind if I bring the little boy on Saturday, ma'am? He'll give me a hand with the watering. The lawn could do with a drop," Gregorio, the gardener, begged her. He dropped back below the ledge and returned to his clipping.

"Yes, I do mind. I mind very much," Elizabeth said to his back. She knew what was behind such requests. It was a way of getting more money and an extra meal. If you didn't put your foot down they'd walk all over you, that's what everyone said.

"I've told you before. Use the sprinkler," she said, clutching her dressing-gown and wishing she'd managed to get herself dressed. Why did Milton take so long in the bath-room?

The cat jumped onto the window-ledge. It brushed against the curtains, arched its back, then disappeared.

It's looking for Matilde, Elizabeth supposed, looking for someone who has nothing to do but toss a ball of wool for it to paw and tangle.

"I'll ask the Mister," Gregorio said.

"Why ask me then?" she said to herself and tugged at the window which refused to shut. She left it open and drew the curtains.

"Tell him to bring the whole family," she felt like shouting across the room and up the stairs." Tell him we'll organize a picnic on the lawn. Or better still a barbecue. What were you saying about the price of meat? Dirt cheap. I know we'll never have it this good again."

And she might have opened her mouth but she realised Milton still hadn't emerged from the bathroom. He thought of it as his own suite, which was as good, if not better, than the tax-free salary that they'd use to pay for James's school, and God knows how many skiing holidays. She felt like throwing one of her books, or better, one of the ornaments from the bookshelves, the clay figure of a woman spinning, or the bronze altiplano church, the green one with the little gold bells that tinkled. A cigarette would do instead. If she wasn't careful she'd bring half the household running. How many of them were there? Whose house was it? If only she had something to read?

She could have pressed the buzzer and asked Matilde to bring her a cup of tea but, more than likely, Matilde was out in the yard, chatting to the washing woman, and handing her bread and coffee, some for herself and some to take away. That, it seemed, was part of the deal. You had to let them fill their pockets, which meant whenever you wanted a snack, there were never any leftovers. As soon as the table was cleared the scraps were whisked away. They went to Matilde, then to the washing woman, then to the garbage women, who threw whatever they didn't want to the ones under the bridge. Nothing, here, was ever wasted.

"Mummy! Mummy! Are you all right?" James pushed open the study door and ran and threw himself on her lap. He was big, for his seven years, and solid. A good eater from birth, they'd let him have what he wanted provided it wasn't junk.

"Of course I'm all right," she said, smiling and stroking his head. "Did you eat your cornflakes?" she asked.

"Mmmmm," he dodged the question, then looked at her with his eyes wide. "Mummy! Can we have rice bubbles next? You could get someone to send them, couldn't you?"

"I suppose so," she said.

"Goody," he yelled and spread out his arms and zoomed

around the room, lifting the top of his pyjamas so that she could see the dark-red welts on his back and stomach. Gingerly she drew him towards her, looked at his body closely, then shrank with despair and anger.

Forgetting herself she ran from the study, across the hallway, and through the dining room, into the kitchen. "Matilde!" she shrieked, wanting help and yet beside herself with distress.

Matilde was a heavily-built girl, aged anywhere between eighteen and twenty-five. Time seemed to stand still for girls like her who left their remote Andean villages, and came to town looking for work, instead of moving into courtship and marriage. The lucky ones were taken in by foreigners, or so they thought, initially, because, as everyone knew, the foreigners had more money; but it was a lonely life. Instead of sleeping under the stairs, or in a boxroom, in the mansions rented to diplomats and engineers, the servants slept in an outbuilding. Furthermore no-one spoke their language, so there was no-one to talk to, most days, but the washing women and, in Matilde's case, the cat.

Matilde had her head bent over the breakfast dishes. Milton's bacon and egg and toast, and James's leftover cornflakes were being scraped into separate buckets beneath the sink. Elizabeth pretended not to see, she didn't care any longer where it went, and so Matilde finished her task. When the girl looked up her face was almost expressionless. Her plaits hung forward onto her apron. With one hand she flicked them back then turned to the bench and went on with her chopping. Everyday, as soon as she cleared the breakfast plates, she began chopping the meat for the midday meal. There it was, on the board, almost ready to be dusted with flour and salt. Alongside the slab there was the pastry. After she'd rolled the pastry, and pricked the pie, she'd begin making the picante sauce.

"James has got ringworm," Elizabeth said, refusing to attempt anything but English, now that she was in such a state.

Staring at the girl she spoke as loudly and as clearly as she could, but, inspite of all the control she now knew she had, her voice shook and she knew Matilde could see she was very upset. For things like that you don't need language. To make her message plain, Elizabeth made a circle with her thumb and forefinger and, twisting her forearm, pressed it against her back and mid-riff.

"James," she repeated. "The cat" then, as if no-one could possibly mistake her meaning, she added, "very sick."

Now it was Matilde's turn to gasp. She put down her knife and, wiping her hands on her apron, went out the back door into the yard.

Elizabeth thought of following her. She would have gone after Matilde but for her dressing-gown. She hadn't meant to sound accusing. She knew how the girl loved the cat. Why had she run off, in a huff, like that?

Upstairs a door slammed. There came a clumping on the stairs. Milton had emerged from the bathroom and was late for work. She thought of calling out to him then wondered, what difference would it make? She'd take James to the doctor and ask the vet about the cat. They must have them here. One thing at a time. That way she knew she could cope. No use letting everything get to her at once.

Looking at the kitchen which seemed so bare and sterile, an empty shell of white tiles and cupboards and food stowed away inside containers, she thought in a way it was almost a relief to have to plan what she would do before her afternoon game of cards. Were they playing today? She must have written it down somewhere. Feeling herself growing more resolute she managed to remember one extra thing. Caught him, just as he was leaving.

"By the way, darling, we're out of Scotch," she shouted through the dining room. "Can you bring some on your way back? I don't especially want to go uptown – the markets and all that."

"I'll send someone from the office. We're finalizing on the Cochebamba-Yungas section today – oh, and, by the way, I'll be at the Club this afternoon, and – the party, don't forget!"

Slam. The front door shut in her face and she found herself in the hallway, staring at the heavy oak panel.

She thought of going after him and telling him what she'd discovered but, instead, she stood quite still and imagined what would happen on the other side of the door. Milton would call Gregorio to open the garage then Gregorio would run and open the gate at the bottom of the driveway. Milton would drive out in the Volvo and Gregorio would lock the gate leaving them secure inside their mansion surrounded by the concrete wall crowned with broken bottles. Here they set the bottles into the cement. Their jagged ugliness was as acceptable in the neighbourhood as the crazed Alsatian prowling on the roof. At least they'd got rid of the dog. It's howling was more than she could stand.

What were they doing here? Elizabeth wondered. Two years ago it had seemed a good idea. The money was a great incentive. It would give them such a boost. And Milton had lost the ashen-grey pallor he usually had at home. But the day seemed like a dark hole in front of her. Should she ring the doctor first? The receptionist probably spoke English. If she went in and showed them what had happened they'd put her at the front of the queue.

When she'd taken James in, for his immunisation, there'd been a man in there bleeding from the anus. The blood was coming through his clothes. She had scarcely dared to look. Nor had she wanted to take a seat. She kept hovering about the desk. Then the doctor came out to greet her himself.

"Senora Mackintosh, how are you?" he'd asked, kissing her on both cheeks and putting her mind at rest with his fautless English. But when he'd led her by the arm she'd felt herself tottering on her heels. As she was ushered inside the surgery, the door closing behind her, she'd looked over her shoulder and seen the sick man standing there, immobile. His eyes were glazed with pain and anger. That was something she hadn't wanted to go through again.

She ran her hand through her hair and thought of going back to the study. It would be nice to curl up with a cup of coffee and let everything sort itself out. She hadn't thought of ringworm, didn't know much about it, but she seemed to recall it was a fungal disease, something you caught from cats. Cats could pass it on to humans, wasn't that it? But Matilde, obviously, wouldn't have had a clue what she was talking about.

"Oh well," Elizabeth thought. Maybe one day she would sit down and learn the language.

The bell, at the gate, began jangling inside the house. Nuisance callers! There was always something. Gregorio would see to them, she thought. Sometimes a tramp, or someone from the other side of the valley, made their way through the tree-lined suburbs, where all the foreigners lived, and stood outside the heavy wrought-iron gates for hours. None of them seemed to want anything in particular. They'd just stand there staring, until you moved them on.

The jangling stopped and the doorbell rang. Elizabeth had no choice but to open it herself. To her surprise it was her neighbour Helen.

"Not dressed," Helen said, with mock surprise.

"Not yet," Elizabeth said flatly, looking at Helen. Track-suit and all. Bouncing around the neighbourhood as if she had nothing to do but think about her figure and the next cocktail party.

"Come in anyway," she said and ushered her unexpected guest towards the study. Then remembered she'd left James in there holding up his pyjamas. For the umpteenth time why did everything have to descend upon her at once? Living here was like child-birth. Some people were cut out for it. They seemed to manage without any fuss. Things went smoothly for them. They weren't, endlessly, being pushed into uncontrollable situations.

"The gate was open," Helen said.

"What!" Elizabeth exclaimed, vexed. "Milton's only just left."

"I know," Helen said, taking the seat by the window and putting her feet up on the coffee table.

Elizabeth pretended not to notice. Instead she pressed the buzzer for coffee.

"I was out jogging," Helen said.

Both of them could hear Matilde calling the cat. Elizabeth turned to the curtains.

"Matilde!" she yelled, but the maid did not appear.

"Giving you trouble are they?" Helen asked.

Elizabeth ignored her. "What difference does it make?" she almost snapped and went to get the coffee herself. When she returned to the study Helen had her nose in a book.

Elizabeth set the coffee-tray on the table and re-fastened the belt of her dressing-gown. Helen smiled as if to say, don't mind me, I'm all right. Then she shifted her feet and asked, "Mind if I close the window."

"I think it's stuck," Elizabeth said, but Helen had already pushed back the curtains and was reaching out for the handle. They both looked out, in the same direction. The shadows had shortened on the grass. Gregorio hadn't shifted from beneath the study window. He was crouched, and clipping the edges. But the focus of attention was not there but at the base of the pines.

James was standing, on the lawn, in his pyjamas and with bare feet, watching and clutching his teddy-bear. Matilde was on her knees. She was facing towards them. The head of the cat was in her lap. With both hands she twisted its neck until the bones parted with an audible crunch. Then she picked up a stone and began hitting the head. Her skirt and her apron were splattered with blood.

"Matilde!" Elizabeth gasped. Pushing away the neighbour, who was clutching her arm, she watched as the girl picked up the cat, with its drooping head, and buried it in a hole in the ground.

The party, that evening, was a glittering affair. The partners had got everyone together to celebrate the signing of the contract for a section of the road to which there was some local resistance. Most of the Anglo-American community were there, including the American Ambassador and his wife, but it was the partners' wives who caught everyone's attention. They looked so glamorous, so exotic.

All that gold, Elizabeth thought. They certainly know how to wear it. They're like peacocks strutting across a lawn, she thought, reaching for another whisky, her third of the evening. But it didn't do the trick. She couldn't join in the chit-chat, with the other wives, about the solar-heated swimming pool, the latest Toyota, the chandeliers at the Hilton Hotel, the gold museum in Bogota, who was seen with who at the Club, the delicious savouries, the maid the Prudencios had.

"It's not as if you'd killed someone," Helen said, her voice barely above a whisper. "Not like the time the people before you, in that house, ran over that girl in their jeep. They had crowds gathering outside the gate. In the end they had to leave. It wasn't safe for them to go anywhere."

"Come on," Milton said, giving Elizabeth a nudge. "This is for us. This is our celebration."

"I didn't know that," Elizabeth said. Her hand was shaking. She reached for a cigarette.

"She was only trying to help," Milton said, trying to calm her down. He wanted her to smile and to play the executive wife. "How'd you like one of those?" he asked, pointing out

the necklace Concha was wearing. "Conchita! You look wonderful!" he called out.

"She wasn't doing it for us." Elizabeth said, not caring who
was listening.

"Forget it," Milton said. "It doesn't matter. You've got to
learn to rise above these things."

"Speak for yourself," Elizabeth said.

Milton was beginning to feel embarrassed. Concha had slipped away instead of coming to give him a kiss.

"Put it this way, she saved you a trip to the vet didn't she?"
he said, trying to cheer Elizabeth.

"Is that what you think?" Elizabeth said, finding herself
looking at him from a great distance. She was feeling light-
headed, delirious, and, yet, incredibly clear-sighted. With that
clear-sightedness came a sense, like a breath of freedom. "You
and your bloody road," she said. "All it is is a way of making
money."

"What are you talking about?" Milton asked, wanting the
floor to swallow him. People were looking sideways at them.
He could see the partners glancing at one another, wondering
if anything were amiss.

"You told me so yourself. You said, for instance, no-one
here knows what to do with the overburden, the mud you
bring down, when you cut, scarring the landscape, burying
villages, forcing people, who live there, to run. You don't care,
you don't think about them."

Milton looked at her incredulously but Elizabeth was taking
in the room, and, trying to regain her sense of balance, walk
a tight-rope, without tripping, a rope strung across a river, a
bridge that had to be crossed.

"Oh do shut up! I thought we were talking about the cat.
What else could she have done with it, for instance?" Milton
asked, trying to look her in the eye, relentlessly, steadily, yet
imploringly.

Elizabeth drew on her cigarette and let the ash fall at her feet. She didn't know. She didn't care. All she wanted to do was pack her bags and run.

"She could have given it to the garbage woman," Helen said, because she was feeling sorry for him.

"Maybe," Milton said, rising to the top again. "At least she could have got rid of it without a fuss." He reached for the savouries and tried putting an arm around his wife.

Elizabeth brushed him away. "No she couldn't," she said, triumphantly. At last she'd understood. Now she could see everything. Now she was on the rope stretched across the valley. "Don't you see," she shouted, so everyone could hear." She's got more brains than you and your consultant engineers could credit. She knew what would happen if she'd given it to the garbage woman. She'd have thrown it in the river and the other ones, they'd have picked it up and eaten it, the ones you can't see, the ones down there, under the bridge."

Suzannah Dunn

MOTHER LOVE

You lie on a table and they spread cold jelly over your stomach; and then a woman comes and sits beside you and slides a bleeper across it. Attached to the bleeper is a machine with a screen at which the woman smiles and points.

"Look," she says, "there's the baby – see? – the head, and the spine."

On the screen something swells in darkness and turns and sinks.

As I lay waiting I heard nurses and radiographers asking questions of their patients: "have you decided on a name? do you want a boy or a girl?"

The woman in the cubicle next to mine told them that it didn't matter as long as the baby was healthy.

I heard the nurses laughing: "healthy? this little one will be playing football for England in a few years' time, you mark my words."

But now, now that it is my turn, no one is laughing. A woman slides a bleeper across my stomach. She stares at the screen; I stare at the ceiling. Eventually she switches off the machine, and rises from her seat.

"That's all," she says.

She asks me not to forget my next appointment with the doctor, and then she leaves the room.

*   *   *

I changed back into my clothes, and caught the bus home. The sky was mottled with cloud but the streets were hot and dry. I walked from the bus-stop at the shopping arcade towards my house. In gardens behind fences transistor radios sang lunchtime radio shows: DJs chatted, quizzed, and chanted their telephone numbers; *get your feet up, girls, and put the kettle on, and here's a mention for all of you in the office...* Their voices came too from inside cars parked at the roadside; cars with windows dropped, doors opened, occupants leaving pastries or sandwiches on the dashboard and heading for the Newsagent. When I arrived at home Jenny wasn't there. Sometimes she stays at college over lunchtime. Next week she will be away on holiday in Corfu with her boyfriend.

She's a young woman now, my husband says, and we can't tell her what she can and can't do.

He will not be here until Thursday. He was promoted recently at work and is required now to spend a few nights away from home each week. I have not yet grown used to it. I had expected to have a little more time with him, not less, as we grew older.

It is hot. The house smells of furniture polish. I opened the door to the garden. Outside it is not yet dark. We lived until recently in the North; and in the North during the summer the sky doesn't blacken at night but flames a deeper blue and melts the sun. The sky in the South is black and sweet at night like chocolate.

Jenny is in the bathroom indulging in rituals behind a closed door. She will emerge cleansed and shaved and deodorized; toned, conditioned, and moisturized; her hair wrapped precariously around her head in a towel. She had always been a grubby child, leaving tidemarks around the bath. I had bathed her every evening during the summer: she had grass stains on her knees and soil under her nails, she looked dirty however hard I scrubbed. She has sallow skin. After her bath each evening I tucked her into her bed, smoothing the sheets around her skinny limbs; her brown wrists and ankles sticking out of the *Mickey Mouse* pyjamas or *Mr Men* nightshirt or whatever else she had chosen the last time we had been to the big stores. When she slept her hair pressed against the pillow smelled of sweet sweat. Jenny never makes mistakes: there are packets of pretty pink pills now in the drawer by her bed.

*   *   *

This morning, before leaving for the hospital, I vomited. I flushed the toilet and dowsed it with bleach but then I vomited again. The vomit slid in streaks down the sides of the bowl. I have been sick every morning for the past three months.

Gastro-enteritis, the doctor said initially, a bug, a virus; and then he had explained the irregular bleeding as a result of my stopping taking the pill.

"Things will take time to settle down," he said.

Pregnancy is the latest of his explanations and as yet I remain unconvinced. I am bleeding still every month, and I never bled when pregnant with Jenny. I never vomited either.

"Things change," the doctor said when I told him, "and all

that was a long time ago."

It was a very long time ago. I told him that I was too old to have another baby.

"Not at all," he said; "lots of women have babies when, like you, they are in their late thirties; in fact, lots of women *start* to have babies when they are in their late thirties."

I started when I was eighteen.

*   *   *

I went shopping with Jenny for maternity clothes: they aren't so hideous these days, she claimed, and there are Young Mum Departments in most of the shops. But this mum isn't so young anymore.

"Very neat," the shop assistants said, "very becoming."

I was forced to parade in front of mirrors; mirrors in front and mirrors behind.

One of the assistants asked if Jenny and I were sisters.

"You look alike," she said

My mother had believed that people were thinkers or doers. Jenny is a doer but I am a thinker. I watched breathless as Jenny scraped through childhood. She mastered all the steps as if they were songs or nursery rhymes, as if she could perform them back to front or standing on her head if she wanted; as if they would have remain with her as snippets hummed from time to time.

People say that children learn by imitation, but Jenny exhibited a precision in her development which belied any haphazard collecting of facts. She understood what made things tick. She was a clever child with clever hands, taking hold of things and taking them apart, unfolding her hands and revealing: *here's a church, here's a steeple*. But she was a thinker, too, in many ways; and she is a thinker still, in many ways, and perhaps more than ever now that she can no longer hop, skip and jump. She was a formidable thinker because she knew exactly what she wanted. She worked through every consequence and complication; she calculated; and all that I ever saw was her winning smile. Her childhood disappeared in a blur of handstands and cartwheels pasted into photo albums. I feel that I have left no mark upon her. She could have been someone else's child. But she is her father's daughter; and he telephoned us this evening after we had returned from shopping but he didn't speak for long as he didn't have much to say.

*   *   *

Today I have been sick all day. I have been in bed. At teatime Jenny tried to make me eat something but I asked her instead for a drink. She brought me iced tea with fruit on top and chunks of ice floating below. When left alone I hear sounds from my silenced radio. Yesterday I mentioned it to my husband when he telephoned.

"It hisses," I said. "It buzzes," he told me; "and it has always buzzed; and if you're worried, you could unplug it."

Today I did not speak to him. He telephoned earlier but Jenny answered and told him that I was unwell and should not be disturbed.

At dusk today I became aware of Jenny at the foot of my bed. I lay still under the sheet and eventually she moved across the room to the window and drew the curtains. When she left I rose and sat on the edge of the bed, listening for familiar sounds. I listened for the Toddler Group mums wheeling their prams along the street, and for the children playing rounders on the green, but I was too late; everyone had gone indoors for the evening. Someone somewhere was washing a car, slopping a sponge around a bucket. It was the only sound. There was nothing else.

I slept for several hours and now I am lying in bed feeling with my fingertips the pulse swelling in my neck. I am sluggish, heavy, constipated, and the baby is still. It has never moved; I have never felt it move. Jenny, however, moves below me downstairs in darkness. She should have gone to bed long ago. She moves slowly from room to room and then she moves back again, retracing her steps. Occasionally she trips and clatters and curses. I should have reminded her to lock the doors and windows because often she forgets. She forgets to unplug the switches too, and one day there will be a fire.

*   *   *

Today Jenny is peculiarly painted. She has told me that she will be going out later this evening, but for now she sits in the kitchen with her father. He returned home earlier this evening. They sit together at the kitchen table in their bath robes. She crosses her legs, and her big toe brushes against the hairs on his leg. When younger she sat for hours with my mother-in-law. The gigantic old lady had been wedged into a wheelchair and covered with blankets; and Jenny clambered into her lap so that with yellowing hands the old lady could stroke her granddaughter's darkly tangled hair. Jenny captivated even then with her mixture of swagger and vulnerability, and for hours the old lady was quietened and would smooth Jenny's hair, gobbling into her ear and spitting her twisted tales and half-digested truths.

*   *   *

They never wanted this baby, Jenny and her father; and babies know when they aren't wanted. They can sense a bad atmosphere. This baby has never moved; I have not eaten for several days; I do not want to grow any larger. My stomach, empty, swells only temporarily. I haven't long to wait now for the results of the scan; the hospital appointment card is balanced on the mantelpiece. This afternoon I sat for a while on the doorstep. Next door there was a paddling pool spread across the lawn. Sunlight reflected on the water. At sunset clouds lay on the horizon like peach slices. I sat on the doorstep and watched the neighbours returning from work. I watched them driving their cars into garages and I listened to them switching off engines and slamming doors. In their houses lamplight sprang in spheres against closed curtains and dropped later into darkness.

Throughout the evening Jenny moved backwards and forwards from room to room across the hall behind me. Once she approached me and placed her fingertips on my scalp before dropping a cardigan into my lap.

"Keep warm," she said.

Then, later, she brought me a herbal concoction in a teapot.

"Drink it," she said, "it'll do you good."

I placed it beside me on the doorstep.

She shrugged. "It won't do you any harm," she said: they were the very words that her grandmother had used many years ago. It was as if she had repeated them, as if she had remembered them; yet she couldn't have remembered them because they had been said before she had been born. I had been pregnant, my skirt stretched tight across my stomach, and the old woman had assumed that her son would not wish to marry me but had smiled nonetheless when introduced. She had smiled in a manner considered appropriate for a woman of her social standing. She told me as soon as we had been left alone together that her son was too young to have a child.

"So you might like to drink this," she said. She handed me a glass of sweet smelling herbal tea. "It won't do you any harm," she said.

And neither did it work.

*   *   *

So in the end the old lady had passed her secrets to Jenny. Jenny is good at keeping secrets. Trustworthy, it used to say on her school reports. Secretive, perhaps. I had waited until I was alone again on the doorstep before tipping the sweet smelling liquid from the teapot to the soil at my feet. Then, eventually, I came into the house. At first we sat here for several hours, Jenny and I, in the living room. She sat opposite me in an armchair. She pretended to read the newspaper. Sometimes her eyes darted towards me, pale and moist and globular like round-bellied fish. Shortly before the rain began she rose to close the window; and soon afterwards, a few minutes before midnight, she told me that she was going to bed. She rose for a second time, and unfolded the newspaper, dropping it behind her into the armchair before leaving. Jenny is secretive: she has a store of secrets, a secret store, because where else are all her hurts and disappointments? On her face there is only that winning smile. She knows so many things, so many, many things about me; she has lived with me for so many years. Traces of her remain here in the room with me: the newspaper, folded; the face powder fallen onto the rug; the pencil slipped among the sofa cushions. Rain slithers across the roof. On the sideboard the pot plants cast no shadow or shade. Despite her smile, her painted smile, my mother-in-law had been a wicked witch with wicked secrets; and now I realise that Jenny has not escaped: I see streaks of it, that wickedness, in my own flesh and blood. But I know what to do about witches, I know how to be free from spells: I must burn everything of mine that she has ever possessed. So all I must do is strike a match and drop it, here, now; and it will be a long time on a night like this before anyone comes running and shouting and trying to discover if there is anyone left inside.

Caroline Forbes

THE WALK

£750,000! All hers courtesy of Littlewood's football pools. The only problem now, she thought, hands dug deep in her pockets, is how to spend it. Well, the first £500,000 could go on buying houses for her friends, perhaps one large block, or a small street. On the other hand they might not want to live that near each other, not all of them. Each one could choose her own. She wondered if she could just hand over the money. Would it be taxed? Did she know an accountant?

She turned the corner of the lane and started out towards the village, head bent against the driving autumn wind that swept across the shorn fields.

She couldn't decide about the car. It would certainly be more sensible to get an estate but then there was the old dream of the red sports car. Maybe she could have both? And the motor bike for the summer? Then there was the washing machine, a new vacuum cleaner and a lawn mower that didn't break her arm every time she tried to start it. So, all in all, about £50,000 for her. Was that too much? Too little? What about when she got old?

She stopped by an oak tree and leant against it for a few moments while two small boys cycled past her sitting back on their chopper bikes and smoking.

She would ask her friends what they wanted, saxophones, tool-kits, greenhouses. Maybe she should save some of the money, set up a trust fund so that there would be cash available every year. Women could apply. She'd better have a P.O. number for the mail. And a committee to decide who got what.

One of the faded green holiday caravans crawled past her. With rain clouds looming on the horizon Mum and Dad were barely smiling and the horse looked bored to tears. As the caravan continued its way to a stopping place on the green in the village she could see two teenage children sitting in the back, legs dangling out, headsets firmly on.

And there would still be £200,000 or so to give directly to her favourite feminist organizations, lesbian ones first of course. She rattled through those that she knew in her mind. But there were probably others, she would have to find out, go up to London and ask around. Perhaps she should send the money anonomously? Or would the women be worried where it came from? Should she just turn up with a cheque book? Would they mind?

A large combine harvester rumbled passed her in the adjoining field throwing up a mist of wheat dust that filled the air while every rodent scurried for cover as it advanced across the field.

Or maybe she should give the money to just a few organizations so that they could really do something with it, rather than spreading it so thin round the country. And what about abroad?

She walked past the mill, pausing as a huge lorry turned out of the driveway with a load of pigfeed bound for Spain.

There were just too many problems. There was one possible solution, she would win £1,000,000 and do a straight 50-50 split. Or maybe better still, she would win the Booker Prize and settle for the £20,000 prize money, the royalties and the film rights. But then she would have to go to the award ceremony. That was fine once she'd decided what to wear, but who should she take? How many guests were allowed? Maybe ten, a nice round number. So then should she take old friends from the past, and if she did would they be offended if she didn't ask their lovers?

She walked round the final bend and into the village. On the green the family had decamped from the fake gypsy caravan and while a blond girl in skin tight pebble washed jeans tried to tether the horse Dad sat and waited for the pub to open.

On the other hand she should ask Julie and Chris and Jan, after all they had put up with her wittering on about the book for the last year. And would the women who published it count as part of the ten or would they have a table of their own? She counted them off in her mind, there would be Sarah, and then Lynn and Mary who with Julie, Chris, Jan, herself and Jo and Pat from the press made up the ten. Or maybe she could have herself AND ten, in which case she could ask Maggie. The rest would have to just not mind, they could be home arranging the party.

Stopping at the post box she extracted the folded envelope from her jacket pocket and dropped it in before setting off up the hill towards home.

It wouldn't go that day, they probably wouldn't get it till Thursday but then they might ring and ask her to come in for an interview. She wasn't sure she really wanted the job, but if she got it she could bear it for a year. And then she could go into business on her own. Or with other dykes. Frances would be good, she lived in Manchester but maybe she could be persuaded to leave. And Rosie, she'd be great at marketing. They could rent one of the new workshops behind the station; at least it would be a place to start. She wondered if they ought to have a receptionist. It would be good if she could persuade Sally Graham to leave her job at the museum and come and join them. But how would Sally react to working with lesbians? Should she be part of the collective?

It had just started raining as she turned onto the track that lead to the cottage. Back on the green Mum had managed to get the stove lit and make a new thermos of tea. The son watched jet fighters wheeling overhead.

And if Frances came, then maybe she would be able to get past her shyness and make something happen. Frances would see beyond her normal burbling exterior to the serious thinking woman within. And Frances would surely be impressed at her winning the Booker Prize. In which case she might have to put off the business for a year to deal with the film rights for the book. She could even take Frances to the States to help decide on the casting. Should she insist on having lesbians play the lead roles? What would she do if Jamie Lee Curtis fancied her? How would Frances feel?

It was Tuesday. She met Lizzie wheeling a barrow load of black rubbish bags down the track to be collected in the morning. She asked Lizzie if anything exciting had happened while she'd been out. It hadn't so she went in to make the tea.

Andrew Garvin

CABINETS

That John McDewell was the worst C.O. I ever had the bad luck to work with at the Department of Health and Social Security, I'm telling you straight. He thought the Department privileged to have him work for it, rather than the other way round. Between you, me and the gatepost, he was doing the Department a big disservice by working as one of its employees. For a start, he was so unpunctual. I know for a fact he didn't possess a clock – he boasted so to Muriel, and she told me. He'd arrive at the office early in summer and late in winter both for the same reason: his up-to-date alarm clock was the sun shining through the patchy curtains of his bedroom. Just marvellous for the Department. Lord help us if the day was overcast. That is, he wasn't technically late, I suppose – if he ever had been I'd have grilled him good and proper and had him for breakfast.

Speaking of breakfast, once when I knew he was going to turn up actually late, I was ready for him, sitting in his place. Everybody stopped their work and stared over at our section, the Special Section. They knew who I was waiting for. This coming and going to and forth was completely undependable, everybody agreed. Nobody else behaved like that. It was upsetting the Section. Even Paddy who knew Nottingham back to front, – so that if a Visiting Officer asked him where Brightside Avenue was he'd reply: "Brightside Avenue? Let's see now, let's get down to brass tacks."

He'd clap his forehead. "Straight up Maid Marian Way on the Tesco side, left at the Co-op, left again at the overgrown garden, full of nettles it's a bloody disgrace! – and Bob's your uncle!"

Yes, even Paddy was that befuddled with all the comings and goings, the unscheduled coffee-breaks, the irregular lunchtimes, that he forgot an address, got his wires crossed between Green Street and Green Avenue, so that the Visiting Officer had to scout around for the map which was three years out of date and didn't show any of the new estates. A downright bloody shambles. So as Paddy looked on with grim satisfaction he gave us a flash of his steel glasses and there was an expectant air all around the office. It even spread to Pension Section, word had got round there, and spilled over into Electricity and Gas Deductions. The H.E.O. Managers were in on it and gave me sly winks and knowing looks over the potted chrysanths Paddy'd brought in, as they carried their coffee in through the main office lined with cabinets the colour of – what? I suppose you'd say sluice-green and the striplight that's been on the blink ever since the S.E.O. tried to repair it with an emergency payment casepaper. The Managers carried their coffee through to their private rooms.

The clock was coming to the last second after which McDewell esquire would be plain late, a serious infringement of the rules of the Service, when we really could throw the book at him. I rang Mr Clarke, H.E.O. on Special Section and asked him if he had time to come through as a witness – he arrived at nine twenty-eight and propped up the Hot Water

Add Back Cabinet.

"When I first came into the Department wet behind the ears," I told him, "I was on five pounds seven shillings and five pence per week after stoppages working from seven in the morning to eight at night with overtime, and I thought I was the cat's whiskers. In my book, Jack, a job worth doing is a job well done. My point is, we were up at six to bus in and thought nothing of it. And now this John comes along with his high-falutin ways and can't get here in time to go for lunch."

"Don't forget, an officer who's almost late is on time, Dick," he smirked back.

"You could just as well say that two and two almost make five." Quite frankly, I'd had doubts about him. He was another one who'd been to university and stuck his nose in the air. Still, not to be backwards in coming forwards, I wanted to keep in with him as he was my Manager.

"With him, it's more likely to make seventeen," I joked, and gave him a beam.

His face cracked slightly. Nine twenty-nine and fifty seconds. We synchronised our watches. In McDewell drifted at 9.30 am with his usual don't-give-a-damn manner at the last second.

"You've only just made it, John, where have you been till this time, would you be so kind as to let me know?"

"Having a big breakfast," he said.

Oh yes, a real clever clogs he was – one of those arty-farty types, his neck had never felt a tie, probably hadn't soap and water either – always wore odd socks, a thin moustache that looked like it had been stuck on at the theatre and never become unglued, face pale as the A14's he made all his mistakes on. He always had some posh newspaper under his arm, coat he swept the floor with, used to shave with a lawn-mower, I think. Or perhaps he used a ginger biscuit. Everyone roared when he came out with that quip about breakfast, even Muriel. I'll settle your hash for you mate, I thought. You're too big for your boots. I'll bring you down to size. Who did he think he was? A two-penny good-for-nothing. Degrees up to his eyeballs and a fat lot of good they'd ever done him – flung out of the Comprehensive for giggling at girls' jokes – or so a little birdie in horn-rimmed spectacles told me – couldn't even teach frog and no better at clerking either. With all those qualifications, you'd think he'd been able to add up. But no, everything had to be turned upside down for John – he did crossed Continental sevens in his hot-water add-back calculations. Immediately, I could tell the book room would take them for fours. I made him go through them all, cross them out, and put real sevens. He handed you a file holding oh so delicately onto the edge, as though it would dirty his hands if he held it any more closely. His file write-ups were the merest scrawl – OK, he could turn out a good minute (that was where his poncified English came in, I suppose), but his worst point of all was his point-blank refusal to work as a member of a team. Now, teamwork is essential to the Section. It's good for morale, it's good for quality. Without teamwork, all putting your shoulder to the wheel, everything goes wrong. But Mr Smarty Pants had to do everything his own way – never mind, of course, perish the thought! – agreeing a lunch rota with Paddy, Muriel or even if it comes to that, with myself – at twelve o'clock on the dot up he shot with – "Well, I'm off to dinner now, Dick. Bit hungry." Hadn't had a big breakfast that day, I suppose. Couldn't fit his lunch break in with the rest of us poor mortals – we all had to fit in with the Great Man's scheme of things, even Paddy who's been with us twenty years and never a murmur except when he laid out an officer behind the counter. (Between you and me, we never mention that on the Section, by the way – Paddy's always had a thing about people who touch his back, lumbago, you see – and what did this officer go and do but brush right against it.)

Now, it's been a time-honoured tradition in our department

that we always put dots, never dashes, in between the numerals of dates. The dot's more economical, it saves time. Upend your biro – and there you've got a clear, unmistakable point. But a dash – a dash is untidy, it can curl upwards, it can turn downwards, it can wave up and down like a lout's shirt tail when the wife tells him he's forgotten to tuck it in the mornings. Of course McDewell, that pain in my neck, was not even consistent about this. Many's the time I've stolen up behind him and watched him over his shoulder: dot, dash, dash, dot, dot, dash, dot. "Very well," I said to myself, "a dash is a stroke that asks to be struck out."

"What's this? Bloody Morse Code?" I shouted in his ear. "Dot and date, John, date and dot it!"

But no, in spite of all my threats, pleas and gentle reminders, we've got our mind on higher things than dots. We like to be different, we think that the dot and the dash are just as good as each other, that both would do equally well and even that the whole matter is rather petty and that there are more important things in the world.

And on top of it all, the lunch at twelve o'clock. So one day I decided to confront John. It was only my duty as Executive Officer to do so. I waited for him to jump up like a Jack-in-the-Box at twelve sharp. Twelve struck, up he went.

"Oh, we're going out to lunch are we, without even so much as a by-your-leave. The whole world revolves around us, John, doesn't it – because we've seen Ken Russell burning down Portsmouth Pier and been to Paris."

Just then, right behind me some brat's voice piped from Public Reception.

"Daddy, daddy, why have we come here?"

"Well, I'll have you know, sonny Jim," I told John, "you're not going to keep on like that working for me. You get an honest penny and do an honest day's work for it here. We must all pull together, work hard and play hard."

"Why, why, why, why!" the father mocked. "Never ask why in life. Never try to know the reason for anything. Then you'll be content."

"Why?" the brat and McDewell chorused together.

"Besides, Muriel," he says (his hackles rising) "didn't Dick agree last month I was to go to lunch at twelve?"

"That's right, Dick," she says, "I remember, it was the same Wednesday my Janet had her wisdoms out."

"Do your one-parent filing, please, Muriel," I says. "Now, look at me, John," I says, "consider me in the midst of your very crowded lifestyle — I go for a half-hour lunch at twelve-thirty, come rain come shine."

"So do I," he answered back with that smirky moustache I'd like to've put through to the back of his head, "only half an hour earlier, as Muriel says we agreed."

"Oh agreed, agreed," says Paddy, on my side, through the potted plants, "but would it be all signed and sealed by Treaty, now?"

"You can set your watch by me, John, or could if you had one," I says.

"I know, Dick," he says, "I've heard you on the phone: 'Could you have dinner ready by five, darling, so that we can have it digested for when we go out.'"

I saw that red bastard had walked halfway past Pensions, before I had time to say anything back. Worse, he'd said it in front of the Clerical Assistants. I swore right there I'd do for him. I shouted down the office: "Where the hell do you think you're going?" Every body looked up from their pocket calculators. "I'm off, Dick," he says. "Never mind," I says. "Try Bella perspiration spray." I laid hold of the drawer handle that hard I nearly tore it off, snatched out his only file, and there and then put paid to that little squirt. Under "Work and Character" I wrote: inaccurate, insolent, insubordinate and insincere. Under "Recommendation for Promotion": demotion? "Oh, so I'm predictable as clockwork am I?" I shouted down the office as he was disappearing past the hat-stands. I went to lunch early, but not before throwing his file into the out-tray for Mr Clarke.

In the afternoon, Muriel was mumbling down the receiver, Paddy explaining why Britain needed a war every ten years to keep it vital, and McDewell dashing and dotting. Everyone on the Section was tense-like after all the argie-bargie. Even worse, a Time and Motion team'd moved in by the hat-stands and were checking the time we took to do the 1979 uprating with Department stop-watches. I tried to break the ice by confiding my wife and I'd decided to stop being egoistic and have a baby, but it was no good. Bold as brass, at half past three, McDewell scrawled his last dash, picked up that damn fool coat which he never hung up on the coat rack, said "Goodbye" and left.

When he'd gone, Jack Clarke, H.E.O., came in with a foul expression, a file under his arm. I knew something was up. Jack lolled up against the L to Z cabinet.

"That McDewell's just left early," I told him.

"I'll have a word with him about it. Be that as it may, Dick," he starts, all hoity-toity, "I've come about something else."

"What would that be, Jack?" I says.

"I'm afraid the tone suggestive of personal animosity towards this McDewell character in your report is not consistent with the high standards of objectivity we like to set ourselves on Special Section."

"Suggestive of" – no word of a lie, he actually said that. He talked like a book, always had done ever since he'd been here. Oh, very lah-di-dah, only been in the job five minutes himself. But I didn't take him seriously.

"Me? Personal animo-what's-it?" I says.

"Why the blue blazes did you have to put all four adjectives beginning with the same prefix 'in' - it sounds so forced, so false," he says. "Besides, 'insolent' and 'insubordinate' mean pretty much the same thing in my dictionary. And what in God's name has 'insincere' got to do with it? Then to cap it all," he says,"you have to go and put a question mark after 'Demotion' which adds to the poor impression of bias, or worse of indecisiveness. I'm sorry, Dick, but I can't authorise this."

I offered to change some remarks, that I'd written.

"No, an eraser would rub a hole in the paper. You've pressed too hard."

"I know, I'll use a snowpake," I suggested. Surely, he couldn't object to that.

"That would be unsightly. It'd look like you were covering up."

I still almost thought he was joking. I offered to write out another, different report. But I noticed his lip quiver. "What do you think we're made of, Mr Groundwell?" he hissed. "Report forms? Did you know that every one of these costs fifty pence?"

I said I'd pay out of my own pocket. "Don't go breaking the rules, Groundwell. You know as well as I do," he says," that money cannot change hands between management officers. It's a matter of ethics. No, I'm seriously worried about you." he stood looking at McDewell's report form for an age. I tried to make out what he was thinking.

He looked up, serious. "Don't think I haven't heard you muttering to yourself on file-searching exercises: 'Sonny Jim', 'clever clogs', 'bitches', and, most mysteriously of all, 'Mr Smarty Pants'."

I swore blind I'd never said any such thing.

"They're terms," he went on, "which might be appropriate to a bar room brawl in a Yates' Wine Lodge, but are scarcely the scientific phrases of dispassionate assessment that are called for here. No, Mr Groundwell, I've decided to transfer you from Monday to the Stationery Department."

And off he stomped there and then, shouting to Muriel to

bring him coffee at four.

Now, ever since last Monday, I've sat in the Stationery storeroom. It's musty with paper and the dust gets up your nose. It's playing hell with my sinuses, I can tell you. Outside, the sky's stuffed with cloud like cotton wool. So what's becoming of me? I feel in prison – yes, imprisoned, I'm not having you on, with vast piles of official forms, and nothing to do but take them out of or put them into boxes. I miss the Irishman's square head and square steel-rimmed glasses, as he talked to me of I don't know what, Howitzer shells, evolution, and the razor-traps he'd put up to catch robbers if they broke in through the skylight of his outside toilet. And the strange thing is, I'm only beginning to realise just how much my hatred of that McDewell helped to pass the time. Ever since that Monday I've sat here wondering: Was I too keen? Wasn't I keen enough? Where did I go wrong?

McDewell passes and waves, cheerily. I make a crack at him, but it doesn't come off, I've not got no heart for it in Stationery.

"Office wit," John says, "is characterised by that sharpness which has been weaned on futility."

Between friends, what do you think?

Rolf Hughes

PROPOSAL

Taking a vacant seat, your eyes are instinctively up-turned, your hands methodically twisting the signs of validity from your ticket, when a hand lands on your shoulder and, with the town slowly rolling again, the smiling face of a former friend appears before you. Preliminaries are swiftly dismissed, then together you pick up the past as if agreed that you have since lived nowhere else. Oblivious of the curious ears of other passengers on the bus which are eager, as always, for anything above the rumbling engine, whining brakes, hissing doors, you seem to recapture in the space of a few stops much of the pleasure of your former friendship.

Then your friend alights and the doors hiss shut. You are alone again, waving goodbye, the smile lingering on your face. She adopts the pose of tragic heroine as the bus moves on, then laughs and waves you on your way. You laugh back in silent dumb show from behind the glass window. "Good-luck!" she mouths and blows you a kiss. The bus turns left and she is gone.

How did you forget her?

Your eyes re-focus on the other passengers who are still watching you with idle curiosity, and you smile a wide smile that spans the entire bus, but your mind suddenly races back over all that has been – now publicly – said, confessed, applauded with knee-slaps of hilarity, and you attempt to gauge from the flat, staring faces whether or not your smile should be given an apologetic twist.

As the eyes turn away, your mouth relaxes and you resume your innocent scrutiny of adverts.

*   *   *

"Ring your parents. They're probably sitting by the phone, waiting for a full report. Tell them to return the cake to the caterers. Tell them to consult the present list, find out who gave what. Then tell them to fetch down all our wonderful crockery and casseroles from their attic and send it back to whoever it came from before they lose their receipts. Tell them the truth – that it's all over!"

"What are you talking about?"

"What am I – ? You should throw up on me – it's the least I deserve."

She was silent for a moment, then replied,

"You shouldn't take everything so personally."

"So personally? Then who else should I blame? The boy that brings the papers perhaps?"

"Don't be silly. Calm down. There's plenty of time to get it right."

Her words stung for they confirmed his suspicions.

"But I wanted to 'get it right' from the beginning. I wanted it to be perfect from the start." He was lying on his side, his words muffled by the pillow which he held over his face. She ignored this latest outburst.

"Don't you see?" he continued. "For it to go wrong now is... is different, completely different. It's no longer the dress rehearsal but the real thing! You must be... devastated. I wanted to make you so happy, and now you must be regretting everything. Why not start again with someone else – before it's too late? Is it too late? Is it? No wonder you're silent. You have already said too much. A couple of words – not even four letters! The longest two words of your life, eh? No wonder you're keeping silent – you see your life hanging in ruins. And guess what? Yes, it's my fault! It is all my fault! I ruined everything!"

He glanced up at her to see the effect of his words. Still her eyes were on the ceiling, still she remained silent. His teeth sank into the pillow in anguish.

"Condemned. By this silence. You are dead to me already. Henceforth my heart is ash."

She sighed, stretched herself and rose from the bed, still without looking at him.

"Really, you're making a lot of fuss about something which is quite unimportant. I do not find you unpleasant, and that – surely – is significant. Let's have no more of this nonsense. Get dressed, let's go down for dinner."

Such heroic, selfless, icy indifference! He was beside himself and for a few moments could make no other sound than an incoherent gurgling into the increasingly-sodden pillow. Then he flew from the bed as if yanked by invisible strings, and rushed at her, his arms waving wildly.

"One more chance! Give me one more chance and I'll make amends! You have yet to see me in my true colours. Forgive, forget, begin again; time will show that you were not so mistaken about me after all!"

"As you like," she murmured, glancing out of the window

as she buttoned her blouse. He started pacing the room, frowning at the carpet before him, utterly lost, it seemed, within the four white walls. She ventured more lingering glances out of the window, for, with her back to him, she could do so without being noticed. Young couples clung to each other by the town fountain, others teased and splashed each other with a sparkling arch of clear water. The noises from the market place floated up to them, but were deadened by the closed window. It was mid-summer, stiflingly hot; the heat and the muffled bustle outside gave the room a certain dream-like quality.

"As you like," she repeated. Back in reply came his quick breathing and the ceaseless swoosh of his bare feet crushing the soft carpet. Distantly, a market vendor started announcing the selling-off of the last of his day's wares in a booming voice that rang in her ears like the mournful baying of an injured animal.

*　　　　*　　　　*

It's your stop. Passengers stare expectantly while you slowly realise this. Even the driver is craning his neck around his partition to watch you. You rise with dignity, saunter along the aisle, and step down beneath the Exit sign. The doors hiss with hostility behind you and the engine rumbles. You watch the bus until it disappears into the horizon, then you cross the deserted road and pass through the park gates.

*　　　　*　　　　*

He hurled the hotel bible at the floor and cried, "Silverfish!"

She turned and saw two, three, then four or five of the tiny insects chasing each other across the carpet. A plimsol skidded across their path, followed by a sandal. He made a dart for the bedside newspaper, swore, rolled it into a club, shouted "Filthy creatures!" and studied the offending area of carpet. The insects scuttled under the bed.

"We must complain to the management. The bed was crawling with bugs – this is really too much!" She was surprised by the sudden age in her voice. "You felt them too?" he asked, studying her.

"I could hardly sleep," she replied wearily.

"So I am not alone after all," he thought, and said aloud, "Good."

She looked at him in puzzlement, but continued brushing her jacket in silence. He was beyond comprehension sometimes.

A sharp tattoo was rapped on the bedroom door.

"Dinner is served in twenty minutes!" The summons was repeated next door, and on down the echoing corridor.

"We must pull ourselves together," he said, running a hand through his dishevelled hair.

She thought of the ritual ahead with an already familiar sinking feeling. What could she find to say to the other guests? So far this day had been as empty as the last. Stooping to slip on a shoe, she glanced at the rolled-up newspaper still in her husband's hand. No inspiration there.

"After all," he continued, "there's no point in making a scene in public. We shall be staying here some time yet, and we can do without the other guests spreading idle gossip about us. Such talk always reaches a waiter or porter or somesuch, and then on to the management, and then who knows what fictitious extra charges will be slipped onto our bill at the end of it all. If only for economy's sake, let us try to behave correctly."

She stared at him. He had become transparent. Only the

second day of their honeymoon – already his head was full of money and his stomach speckled with ulcers. Contempt flashed across her face.

Once again there was a sharp knock at the door, but without the summons. He turned to her, seeking her eyes for guidance. Only then did she realize that he was still naked. She shrugged.

"One moment!" he called out in an uncertain voice. Again the knock – more impatient.

"One moment!" he shouted louder, looking desperately around the room for his clothes. How little time it takes to get to know someone, she reflected as she watched him panic.

The door flew open.

"Good evening, good evening, good evening! We were beginning to think you had gone out to the theatre, where everyone else seems to be tonight – although why, when we have each other to entertain and be entertained by, I cannot imagine. Or else, that we were – ha,ha,ha! – knocking at an inopportune moment. That's not the case, is it darlings?"

Her father, grinning ferociously, stood at the head of a group that had marched into the room, and which consisted of her family, their neighbours, the local parish priest, and an ex-lover. The mother fixed her weepy grey eyes on her daughter and took a tentative step forward.

"My poor girl! What has he been doing to you?"

The parish priest genuflected at the sight of male nudity.

"We noticed you were in," the first neighbour chirped, her lipstick stretching far across her face in a beatific smile of happiness, "by your curtains. They were closed earlier, and quite right too in this heat –"

"Don't be pushed around," her elder sister recited dispassionately. "Stand up for yourself – have pride – fight back."

The ex-lover stood at the back of the assembled group, content to merely smile at her and waggle his eyebrows suggestively from time to time.

Their sudden appearance did not cause her the slightest alarm. She gazed at them with mild interest for a few moments then commented,

"Your patience is remarkable. Anyone else would have hopped along after a couple of knocks."

"You have always known your family to be patient," the priest intoned, "supportive of its members, forgiving them their erring ways —"

"Well, I'm glad we've caught you in anyway," her father continued, while the priest cast his eyes heavenwards at the possibly blasphemous interruption. "And in such good health — because, you know, without good health nothing really tastes of much and tonight I have it on good authority they have lobster on the menu." He waited for a response, but his daughter stared blankly at him and his newly-acquired son-in-law was busy trying to hide behind a sheet of yellowing paper on which was printed the hotel's fire regulations. The sister turned to him.

"What are you hiding from us?" she demanded in a monotone.

"We heard your outburst," the priest turned his head in the bridegroom's direction, but kept his eyes piously averted. "You've read one too many Russian novels, haven't you?"

The young man said nothing and there was a brief silence as the assorted company gathered their assorted thoughts. The mother dabbed her eyes with a dusty handkerchief. A round of muffled laughter and applause came up from the outside street.

"Glorious day!" shrieked the second neighbour, pulling a steam iron from an inside pocket and waving it wildly overhead. "Real drying weather!" She frowned at her feet for a moment, then looked up and added, "And about time too!" By way of emphasis, a tremor rippled her sagging cheeks.

The father's gums were turning white around the teeth from

the pressure of his unwavering smile.

"Yes, it's lovely to find you both here," he continued, "when everyone else seems to be racing out to the theatre, or the opera, or whatever it is they're foresaking the worthy lobster for..."

"You will tell your mother everything, dear, won't you?" A tear trickled from her mother's left eye, while behind her the ex-lover's eyebrows performed gymnastics of suggestivity.

"... We've had a most pleasant afternoon looking around this little honeymoon town of yours and there's much to talk about. And so I have taken the liberty of procuring from the downstairs bar... a bottle of the excellent local red, a '79... Tara!" And, pausing only to wipe a speck of spittle from his bloodless lips, the father produced the bottle from an inside pocket with a flourish.

"Don't mind if I do!" chorused the collective neighbours in feigned surprise as they moved in. An elderly couple linked arms in anticipation and performed a slow-motion jig towards the bottle.

"Have you any glasses?" the father asked, gliding away from them and across to the bedside table. "I'll soon have it open – I carry my own corkscrew all the time. It's part of this Swiss Army penknife which my Godmother gave me on my fourteenth birthday and which I have carried with me ever since..." He held it up for all to admire. "... Except, of course, in bed or in the shower – ha,ha,ha! Good God! Is that a silverfish on the table? It is! And look, a couple there, on the carpet, how disgusting! I must leave you. I can't abide the creatures. Insects of any description make me queasy." He started edging towards the door, the bottle still in his hand. "I think... we best... carry on this conversation... downstairs... in the restaurant." So saying, he turned and fled from the room, closely followed by the assorted neighbours, the genuflecting priest, the sister, her tearful mother, and, with one last grin and waggle, the ex-lover.

Daughter and sister, former parishioner, neighbour and ex-lover, now reached under the bed and pulled out the marital suitcase. She threw some folded clothes towards her husband, who was still standing trembling in the corner of the room, smiled fondly at him, and said at last,

"Come on, get dressed. Let's go out the back way and find a restaurant a long, long way from here."

*   *   *

You walk over the heath, glorying in sunshine, long-remembered tunes, cherished scenes from the ever-changing film library that is your past. Your steps meander from the path onto the newly-cropped grass, and, were it not for a faintly-recollected rendezvous that might be responsible for your being in this particular part of the world at this point in history, you would curl up in the sun and watch the seasons pass through the trees and the hair float from your scalp with complete indifference.

As it is, there are people who rely on you. Perhaps you rely on them relying on you? Anyway, they won't leave you alone; even alone on the heath they are with you, before your eyes, pulling your dawdling steps onwards. You attempt to banish them for a moment by flooding your skull with music. A light breeze is rustling the foliage on the heath. Pairs of dogs are whirling in circles as they attempt to sniff each other. Old individuals and young couples sit similarly glassy-eyed on benches. Children gurgle, chase kites, clap hands or shout "It's all dead!", while a solitary parent shelters inside her overcoat, dreaming patient dreams and looking like a lone sapling on the rolling expanse of parkland.

And you are hearing a tune you've long grown out of, one

you thought dead and buried beneath the topsoil of adolescence
– a pop tune, as they say, of yesteryear, by which certain aims
were reached, but aims that now seem far from certain. With
the melody comes the memory of a garden, open French windows, a blue batik headscarf, the shadow of curls on a sun-tan-
ned neck... Your thoughts are suddenly sabotaged by the jingle
of a perfume advert. You shake it from your head with annoyance and venture into the next dimly-remembered verse.
She eludes you, she still lacks a face and personality in your
blurred memory. Back to the chorus, you hum it aloud and
hang on each note, possessive of the calm sensations that are
suddenly resurrected; a summer breeze gently rustling the
leaves of potted plants, drowsy laughter rolling around the
warm room, and the steady, surreptitious pressure of a thigh
against yours on a piano stool... Her features slowly surface
in your thoughts and you can see her long fingers poised above
the black and white notes of the keyboard. You replay an inept,
impromptu duet which dissolves into laughter. There is a ring
on her left hand. You laugh louder. She leans against you.
Everything around you is indescribably funny. Her thigh is
warm against your own. Your mouths move – Suddenly you
are both silent, separate, sitting straight, trying the duet once
again, but seriously this time; her husband has returned with
a tray of drinks and is smiling indulgently at his clever musical
wife. The prim duet echoes and fades. You release its empty
notes on the breeze, and then the all-too-living phantoms of
those who rely on you, expect things of you, expect you at this
very moment (you check your watch – you are late already),
rise up with eyes full of wounded love, and you see yourself
with ghastly clarity; a solitary figure, humming tunelessly to
itself, crossing the park in aimless zig-zags.

You shade out this vision, and into focus falls a distant
"Wall's Ice Cream" sign, tin, waving in the wind. A mark of
a world you thought would not intrude on the heath. The sign

heralds a cafe – empty – which in turn recalls you to the world of greetings and meetings and all the welcome rituals of companionship. Far beyond the sign, a flock of birds rise wheeling into the sky, corkscrewing higher and higher until, barely visible, they hang in the air, a cloud of black pepper on a pale blue expanse, preparing to migrate, waiting for late-comers. You watch them for some minutes, the cloud expanding and contracting as the birds circle, swoop, and soar in the air. Then they disperse and slowly, separately, come spiralling down to your spinning patch of heath; a trial run, mere preparation, a false alarm. You look away as the "Wall's Ice Cream" sign turns a somersault in jubilation, and step, with resolute step, down the gently sloping path at the fringe of the dark, condom-strewn forest; suddenly your arm is seized and there is hot breath in your ear, forming itself into the syllables, "You're late!"

*   *   *

He sat in the court with his head bowed as the final witness was summoned, sworn in, and positioned in the dock.

"You are the father?"

"I am."

"You have heard the evidence?"

"I have."

"Will you give the court, in your own words, your testimony of the events which led up to the disappearance of your daughter?"

"With pleasure, Your Honour." The father took a sheaf of papers from his jacket pocket, put on his spectacles, and cleared his throat. He then smoothed out his statement and read the following words in a loud, ringing voice.

"No-one could conceivably fault the warm hospitality with which we welcomed my daughter's husband into our family on the occasion of their wedding. Our family has always been close, 'supportive of its members, forgiving them their erring ways' as the good Reverend has testified. We were therefore happy to abide by whatever decision our darling youngest girl made respecting her future life. Such reservations as I confess we had as to her choice, we kept strictly to ourselves. We did them proud on the day, and there wasn't a dry eye in the family as we waved them off on their honeymoon.

"We've never been without her before, and so we asked her to phone as soon as she landed to tell us she had arrived without trouble, and then as often as possible so we could be reassured that she was coping on her own. Honeymoons are worrying times, Your Honour, for bride and parents alike. To add to our anxieties, they had chosen to honeymoon in a foreign country, where the climate and diet were not what she's used to and where few would have the intelligence to speak English. And so, when a couple of days passed without a word from her, we started worrying in earnest. We knew that our girl would not simply abandon us once she had left the country, nor could she lose herself in any young man so far as to forget those that always come first in her heart. So we decided to fly out on the next flight.

"I understand, Your Honour, that you are a father yourself. Forgive my impertinence – I am unpracticed in the learned ways of our fine courts – but I beg you to imagine with me, for a brief, harrowing moment, the feelings of grief, of disgust, and finally of rage that every father must share at the thought of someone... tampering with his daughter. Marriage is not an issue here – it is the despoliation of all he holds sacred in his heart. His own flesh-and-blood can never again be the same. I believe you understand me, Sir. I shall continue.

"Who could conceivably call into question the gracious

generosity with which my family extended the olive branch to my daughter's husband that same night by inviting him to join our little dinner gathering? Nonetheless, no sooner had we settled at table, eagerly anticipating good company and hearty local fare, then we spied him skulking down the staircase with my daughter, evidently with the intention of leaving the hotel and giving us the slip. My wife and our eldest daughter rushed across, hailed them, and reiterated our desire to dine with them. I made a point of rising to greet the boy with a warm handshake, personally hanging up his jacket, and sitting him down, all the while keeping up a friendly patter of pleasantries calculated to put him at his ease.

"The erudite Reverend and myself had been discussing ancient civilizations at the table; the Aztecs, the Incas, the proud Mayas, and the Chibcha of Columbia. Since my son-in-law is apparently incapable of earning a wage, I assumed that like one or two of these over-educated types, he would at least be good dinner-table company, at least able to contribute his own observations to the conversation, which was general in nature. Instead, he sat in our midst in what I can only describe as sullen silence. Some drunk was holding forth from the bar – not exactly improving our image abroad, Your Honour, flying off to the Costa del bloody Dole and running riot in bars with their giros, pardon my French. His obscenities were evidently more entertaining to my son-in-law than the conversation around the table. My daughter was also untypically subdued, and despite the worthy priest switching the conversation over a range of topics – including, for her benefit, childrearing, domestic management and the rhythm method – we were hard pressed to get a single word out of the pair of them. Rum company, Your Honour, after one has just flown across Europe to dine at the same table! Nonetheless, we made the most of an excellent dinner, little realising that it would be the last complete family gathering.

"It was while we were tucking into dessert – slivered pears, smothered in cream and topped with walnuts – and I was contemplating what sort of future my daughter had made for herself, that the accused – I should say the accursed wretch in the dock there! – suddenly thrust back his chair, hurled his spoon to the floor, and accused me of snobbery in regards the lower orders – I, who have organized so many charity functions in our neighbourhood and who had the good grace to sacrifice my prettiest girl's prospects to this penniless, prospectless wretch simply because she assured me that it was what she wanted at the time. I was too shocked to speak and could only watch as if in a dream as he then turned on my daughter, his wife, and charged her with failing to admire the culinary acrobatics of the chefs behind her; framed by a narrow serving hatch, they were spinning elastic circles of dough high in the air, deftly catching them, and then pouring on the ingredients that created the flavours for which their pizzas are famous. My daughter protested her innocence, pointing out that her back was turned to the serving hatch so how on earth could she be scorning something she couldn't see? But he would not listen to reason. He lunged forward, seized the serving bowl, scooped up handfulls of pears, cream, and walnuts, and pelted the very family to whom he'd so recently had the audacity to legally align himself. His laugh, Your Honour, while he performed this unspeakable insult was nothing short of insane. Sad to relate, my daughter was also laughing – but for her it was the hysterical reaction of shock. What shameful behaviour for a girl to endure before her parents – and on her honeymoon too! When the brute had emptied the bowls and while the drunk at the bar was doubled-up in disgusting Northern laughter and we were sitting in grim silence, dripping with expensive dessert, my daughter stood and embraced her monstruous husband. This nearly moved me to tears. She became a Saint and an angel for me from that moment. Is there no end to her self-sacrificing goodness? There is certainly, however, no end to that creature's depravity; he shook her off and muttered something about her being better off amongst her own – truer words never issued from his rancid lips – before seizing my bottle of Chianti, snatching his jacket from the hook and storming out of the restaurant without leaving the smallest contribution for the food and drink he'd just squandered or stolen.

"The rest is known to you, Your Honour. You have heard the testimonies of the priest, of my good lady wife and our remaining daughter, of Mr and Mrs Spickle and of the Bocton household, all highly-respected members of the community and pioneering lights in our Neighbourhood Watch schemes. You have heard police reports, school reports, and now my report – all of which corraborate the evidence and point to an inescapable verdict.

"We had seen enough nonsense over those two hours to know that our girl was better off with those who truly loved her. We packed her suitcase without further delay, and took her in a taxi to the airport and from there back to her own country and back to her own home. She was tired and upset of course – who wouldn't be? – but a few good meals from her mother and the love and care of her family and, by the grace of God, we soon had her right as rain.

"Your Honour, forgive these foolish tears. They spring from a father's broken heart. On the morning of the eleventh I took her her morning cup of tea. The room was empty, her things gone and the note that was earlier read out in court was left on her empty pillow. 'Don't try to trace me' – that's what brings on the tears.

"Be not surprised that she is not to be found in this brute's hovel, for she is not of the mettle to suffer fools gladly. She has either escaped already, or – God forbid – is lying trussed up and drugged somewhere in harsh captivity. I believe, however, that she is free, and is hiding out of shame – yes, shame!

– for this monster's disgraceful behaviour to her own beloved father. All who know her believe that our darling, beautiful girl was bewitched by the creature in the dock before you. We believe – and Almighty God bear Witness we do so from the eternal love in our hearts! – that he insinuated his way into her affections without her conscious consent. He has, you will agree, the air of the hypnotist about him – even at this moment. Common sense dictates the verdict of a just jury – their foolish marriage must be annulled at once and steps taken to prevent him ever again taking possession of my daughter's body and soul..."

"Lies!" he cried, rising to his feet. "You stifled her at birth!"

"Silence!" hissed the judge.

"Scum!" shouted the father.

"Scum, scum!" bayed the public gallery.

"I haven't seen her, I haven't seen her!" he wailed, sinking to the floor. The jury lowered their eyes as a wave of yawning swept them. The judge rapped his knuckles on his mahogony desk and they promptly pronounced "Guilty" in unison. The judge nodded his assent and ordered the prisoner to stand to hear his sentence.

"You have been found guilty by a court of law of disrespect to that court of law, disrespect to legal kith and kin who spared no effort in offering you the laurel wreath of hospitality in a foreign land, and of cynical disregard for your marriage vows by causing the disappearance, in a wilful and premeditated manner, of your lawfully-wedded wife. What is your sentence?"

"I always loved her." he stated with care.

"How sentimental!" returned the judge, pulling a cigar from his trouser pocket, lighting it, and leaning back to enjoy his favourite part of the session. "Hackneyed, predictable, and, I might add, utterly unconvincing. Now you may sit to hear my sentence."

The prisoner sat as the judge puffed contentedly for a few moments before vociferously clearing his throat.

"In the light of the evidence and of the just verdict of the jury of this court of law," he intoned behind clouds of smoke, "and according to the authority vested in me by the Attorney General and Chief of Justice –"

A woman's voice rang out from the gallery.

"Shut your mouth and give your brain a chance! I've heard more sense from a pack of bloody poodles!"

"Remove that woman." barked the judge, but the ushers had already seized her arms and were bustling her from the court.

"And as for the clown with the long face and stomach-churning sermon... Body and soul? My arse!"

They hauled her up the steps to the door, but she swung her legs into the air and planted her feet firmly on the sturdy double doors.

"She's alive... and kicking..."

Her legs were forced down and the doors were opened.

"... if only you listened to her story instead of playing ping-pong with her memory..."

The doors slammed shut on her words.

The judge took a sip of water and continued, with admirable professionalism, from where he had left off.

" – having considered the severity of the crime, the grief inflicted on the victim's father, and your wilful indifference to legal affairs as manifested by this offensive slouching as I speak to you, it gives me great pleasure to sentence you to profound pain in the privates in the specific form of testicular pulverization, the punishment to be prolonged in a public place for a duration deemed decently desirable."

He collapsed onto his knees applauding the judge's alliteration, and a chant of "Unto death!" thundered from the public gallery.

*   *   *

"You're late!" she says, seizing your arm from behind, whispering close into your ear, and laughing as you start with surprise.

"You're late, I've fought off hunger pangs, walked around the lake twice and even had a go on a little girl's sailing boat. I almost stood you up – it's the least you deserve. Where were you going with such a solemn expression? Not coming to meet me, I hope?"

She twists your ear as she teases you, then brushes her lips across your cheek.

"I'm sorry," you say. "I was on my way. I fell asleep on the bus, had some ridiculous dreams, and I only woke up at the stop by the far gate. Isn't it glorious out?"

"Real drying weather," she replies. Her eyes meet yours.

"As they say," she adds. She looks away and laughs.

You slip your hand into her coat pocket, her palm presses yours and your fingers intertwine.

"More like walking weather," you say. "Let's go and get something to eat at a restaurant a long, long way from here."

"But I'm starving!" she protests. "Let's go to the nearest place we find, otherwise..."

You walk hand in hand down the hill, pretending to argue and now playfully trying to push each other off the path. The sun is nailed in an eternal sky.

"Marry me," you say, on impulse.

Saul Hyman

REMEMBRANCE DAY

The newspaper was sticking through the letter-box in the front door when Richard came downstairs. The thick Sunday papers wouldn't fit through the slot. Breakfast would take too long if it included the papers so he left them in the door. He made the coffee and took it upstairs to Cathy. She was still fast asleep but she woke up when she smelt the coffee.

Everything was loaded into the car and the front door was locked when he tried to pull the paper out of the letter-box. Pulling it from the front did not work – he just tore the front page. Swearing, he unlocked the door and pulled the paper through from the inside. Then he saw the small, grey image of his father's face smiling weakly from the torn front page. *Jackie Prescott remembers Henry Dawson* announced the headline. He put the paper on the back seat of the car and caught another glimpse of the wan smile as he reversed out of the tight parking space. He cursed the neighbours for parking so close. Driving through the streets of south London he felt his father's face staring up from the back seat.

He had taken the photograph on his father's last birthday. They went for a walk together after lunch – one of the few times he could remember being alone with his father. His mother enlarged the photograph and put it on top of the television in the sitting room. Had she given it to the newspaper?

As he reached the motorway Richard wished he had brought his sunglasses. When they left the flat it did not look as if the sun was going to come out. Cathy never left the flat without her sunglasses; they must be in the bottom of her handbag. He could wake her up and ask her to take them out. He could just pull off the road and search in the handbag himself.

The sunshine made the autumn leaves a rich brown and yellow. The city was grey and black; brown was last year's colour. As a child he stared out of the back window of his parents' car at the rushing fields – trying to remember the route in case they got lost on the way back. Richard was driving so fast he nearly missed the turning off the motorway. His sudden braking woke Cathy and she gazed bleary-eyed out of the window as they drove slowly through the narrow streets of the village.

He had forgotten the name of the pub in the village. What was it called the Wheatsheaf – the Harrow? Something agricultural. He used to play on the swing in the garden. Maybe the publican would remember him? Pink bald head and glasses – Eddie – that was his name. Now that the new shopping centre had been completed the pub was a thatched oasis in a plate glass desert. The Plough, that was its name.

Since his last visit the Plough had been taken over by one of the large breweries. Eddie and the swing had gone: video machines and fizzy beer had arrived. They found a table next to where the open fire used to blaze.

"I'll have the ploughman's and a G and T."

Rubbing against the bar he waited for the barmaid's attention. It was just the right height. She was pretty, blonde, good figure. She kept smiling at him. A box of plastic poppies got in his way when he tried to pick up the drinks. With a final smile the barmaid gave him the drinks and a plastic token with the number seven on it. He put it in his jacket pocket and dribbled back to the table with a pint of lager and a gin and tonic. Cathy put down the newspaper and inspected the food.

"Did you see the thing about your father in the paper?"
"Just the usual rubbish I expect."
"There's a good photo of him... Oh Richard!"
"What is it?"
"You didn't get me a poppy?"
"You don't want one of those?"
"Yes I do, everyone's wearing them."

Fearful of encountering someone from the past, Richard had not looked round the bar when he arrived. Pulling the token out of his pocket he ran his finger along the groove of the seven. Casting a furtive glance around the pub, he was relieved that there was no one he recognised. Most of the other drinkers wore the red flowers. A group of young boys played the video machines. They weren't wearing poppies.

"Not everyone's wearing them."
"Come on Richard, don't be such a spoil sport."
"What's the point?"
"It's a way of remembering those who died in the war."

"Well I wasn't around then and I don't need plastic flowers to help me remember dead people I've never known."
"OK, cool it, I didn't realise it was such a big issue. Isn't that our number?"

The bar seemed a long way away. Above the babble of voices and the haze of smoke he distinguished the number seven on the distant screen. Elbowing his way through the tweed jackets and green wax anoraks he eventually reached the bar. Richard felt the barmaid deliberately avoiding his gaze. Tapping the plastic token on the bar attracted her attention and she went to fetch the food from the kitchen. As he waited for her to return he slotted a coin into the plastic box and picked up a poppy.

Cathy put the poppy in her hair and poked at her food. She read the colour supplement whilst he read the newspaper. There was a large version of the picture inside. Richard looked furtively at the photograph of his father as if he was taking a surreptitious glance at a picture in a pornographic magazine – an image of an emotion he could no longer share. He had taken the photograph when they reached the top of the cliff; his father smiling and laughing. The grey, grainy image reduced the laughing, frowning face to a polite grin. He started to read the article.

> "In this exclusive extract from her forthcoming biography of Henry Dawson, Jackie Prescott describes the last days of television's medieval mystery man. Formerly Professor of Medieval Literature, Professor Dawson became known to millions of viewers through his regular television appearances..."

Further down the page he saw several other pictures of his

father with C.S. Lewis and J.R.R. Tolkien – photographs which had stood in his father's study for as long as he could remember. He heard Cathy put down the colour supplement.

"Hey are you going to spend all day reading the paper? We'd better hit the road if we're to reach your mum in time for tea."

In the car Richard turned on the radio in search of some lively music. His mother always objected to pop music and he needed to hear some now.

> "... *and thou shalt visit thy habitation, and shalt not sin...*"

All he could get on the radio was the church service. He turned the radio off in annoyance.

*   *   *

When she sits at his desk, Dorothy feels as if Henry might walk through the door at any moment. The window in front of the desk looks onto the shrubbery. The envelope from the hospital lies on the desk; as she picks it up Henry's wallet, cheque book and credit cards tumble out. The wallet contains the passport photographs of a bashful young woman with long hair – that was how he remembered her. From his desk Henry watched her as she weeded and pruned, still harbouring his passion for the young woman smiling shyly in the photograph. She bends and twists the credit cards until a white plastic scar appears down the centre and then cuts them in half with the embossed scissors he bought her in Italy.

Widowhood is a very long weekend. Another Sunday without husband or son. No one to argue with about the washing-up, no one to appreciate the million martyrdoms which for more than a quarter of a century made up a marriage. She turns on the wireless.

> "... *thou shalt know also that thy seed shall be great, and thine offspring as the grass of the earth. Thou shalt come to thy grave in a full age, like as a shock of corn cometh in in his season...*"

Dorothy cuts the photograph into little pieces. They drop like confetti into the wastepaper basket. She will never again look young in anyone's eyes. Dorothy turns off the service from the cenotaph and pushes aside the pile of unopened letters on the desk. Looking through the windows at the garden, she sees the sun trying to break through the clouds.

Behind her the bookshelves of the study are mute witnesses. The serried ranks of the Early English Text Society form a miniature stonehenge. Henry's own books – rigorously examined variant readings obtained from obscure manuscripts have a shelf of their own. Products of a lifetime spent assessing allegorical imagery and elucidating the ambiguity of the medieval text.

She closes the door reverently and walks slowly up the stairs. In the bedroom Henry's bed lies next to hers, the bedside table separates the two expanses of cream candlewick. Inside the cupboard a dark regiment of suits stands to attention, beneath them parade massed ranks of shoes, rigid with shoe trees.

The cupboard under the stairs is the home of the bin liners.

Dorothy selects the largest, strongest bags she can find. They are made from heavy duty green plastic and are usually reserved for compost. Today they have a different destination.

Slowly and deliberately, she ascends the stairs and returns to the bedroom. The bin liners gradually assume a shape of their own as she fills them with Henry's suits. Before folding them, she checks the pockets, amassing a collection of train tickets and scraps of paper.

The cupboard is nearly empty when Dorothy puts her hand in the pocket of Henry's favourite tweed jacket and finds his pocket diary. Richard always buys him the Anglers' diary for Christmas – although it was years since he went fishing. The first half of the year is full of creased pages with methodical lists of all the tasks which have to be done. From May onwards the pages are clean and empty. There were not many engagements to cancel. Death is a month without appointments. She sits down and scans the empty pages of the diary – searching the crisp white spaces for clues as to Henry's whereabouts.

The tears are pricking behind her eyelids as she looks with satisfaction at the cupboard liberated from Henry's suits. Then she remembers the chest of drawers is still full of his socks and underpants. The carrier bags hang from a peg above the cardboard boxes in the cupboard under the stairs. She fills one bag with socks and another with underpants. In the small top drawer she finds his hairbrush and comb. His white hairs still cling to the brush. Summoning every last ounce of will-power she deposits the brush and comb in the sock bag.

When the drawers are empty she dusts them out, re-lines them with paper and colonizes them with her underwear. At the bottom of the stocking drawer Dorothy discovers an old packet of cigarettes. Henry gave up smoking and coffee when Doctor Walker diagnosed his heart condition. She used to indulge after a good meal but she has not smoked regularly for years; it seemed churlish to indulge in pleasures Henry could not share.

In the lounge, Dorothy puts on her favourite Beethoven piano sonata and makes a pot of real, strong black coffee. Then she lights a cigarette. The coffee tastes bitter – the unaccustomed smoke makes her cough, but the music sounds sweet. Excited by her recklessness, suddenly able to do exactly what she wants – she no longer knows what that is. What would Henry think if he came in and found her smoking?

When the door-bell rings, she stubs out the cigarette like a guilty school girl. She is not expecting Richard yet; it's not like him to be early. Geoffrey's ruddy face beams through the little window in the front door. Catching sight of her face in the hall mirror she looks flushed. She does not want anyone to see her like this.

"Dorothy, I was expecting you for lunch."
"Oh goodness, Geoffrey, it quite went out of my mind."

She feels herself blushing.

"Are you alright?"
"Yes, I was just sorting through the letters. Richard's coming down this afternoon and I forgot all about lunch... I'm sorry... Could you have a quick look, so I know what to give Richard?"

Dorothy guides Geoffrey into the study. He slips easily into the swivel chair while she sidles into the sitting room and steals the ashtray into the kitchen. When she returns with the tea Geoffrey asks her questions about insurance and dividends and probate. A thousand questions which she cannot answer. His explanation makes her feel even more dependent. He is full of what he is going to do for her, he knows so-and-so who will do such-and-such. Henry told her that Geoffrey would look after things.

"Do you want to come over for a quick bite to eat?"
"No thank you, I'm really not hungry and Richard and Cathy will be here soon."

As Geoffrey leaves she wants him to hold her, to reassure her that life will return to normal. He leaves her with a quick peck on the cheek and the lingering feeling that she is slowly moving from friend to obligation.

She wishes she had asked him to take her into town but she cannot bring herself to make further demands on him. Anyway she can get what she wants from the village shop. The walk will do her good but it is so expensive in the village and she has to watch the pennies now. She goes into the garden but the tranquillity which she usually finds is not there. Occasionally she turns round feeling that someone is watching from the study.

*   *   *

"We should get some flowers for your mother."
"Is it really necessary?"
"I'm sure she would appreciate it, Richard."

Cathy put the gladioli on the back seat and they drove off in silence.

"I wanted to get another bunch but I thought you'd probably complain."

"More than one bunch?"

"You haven't seen your Mother in months and then all we bring her is one rotten bunch of gladdies."

"I have other ways of showing my affection."

Cathy pulled down the sun visor and fixed the poppy to the strip of elastic across the corner of the plastic flap. Staring at the tiny oval mirror, she put purple lipstick on her lips. Attaching the poppy to the car was her revenge for not being able to stick it through his buttonhole.

Cathy was painting her nails. He was not sure if she was listening to him. Sometimes she encouraged him to talk about his parents and then switched off. She said it was important for him to get his feelings out of his system but at the moment painting her fingernails was more important.

The smell of the nail varnish annoyed him. They would be there in a minute. Why did she always choose the wrong moment to do these things? He braked suddenly and she cursed him.

His mother took a long time to answer the door bell. She must be in the garden. Richard suddenly remembered the last time he sat in the garden. It had been his father's birthday – the summer before he died. His mother was clearing up the birthday lunch. The two men were sitting in the garden when his father suggested a walk on the beach. The tide was coming in as they walked up to the cliffs – water swirling around great chunks of rock in the sea. They should have been sensible and waded back through the water. Suddenly they were daredevil kids climbing up over the sheer cliffs – the camera dangling round his neck. Sheer madness, terrifying when he looked back. When they reached the top he took the photograph. His father looked flushed after the steep climb. A rare moment – the unguarded image – his father laughing with his eyes as well as his mouth.

"Oh, what lovely flowers, you shouldn't have."

Parents are like television celebrities; they look older and smaller in the flesh. Dorothy seems to have shrunk since he saw her last. The peck on the cheek is lighter; the frown on her forehead is deeper.

"Could you reach down the vase from the shelf for me? I'm not as young as I used to be."

The appearance of a man obliges Dorothy to assume a temporary helplessness. She always asks Richard to do something for her when he arrives. The vase was a wedding present. His mother returns from the kitchen with the vase full of water.

"I don't know how you can bear all the noise of the city."
"It's where the work is."
"So everybody says. There's nothing round here. All you young people have moved away..."
"Mum you're starting to sound like an old woman, 'all you young people'."
"Well I'm not getting any younger. Shall I make the tea? They really are lovely flowers and they look just right in that vase."

She had had the photograph enlarged, taking the private moment between father and son and putting it above the television set. Now the vase of gladioli occupies its place.

Richard walks into the study. There are neat piles of opened letters on the desk. No monochrome pictures lean against the spines of the books on the shelves. He has a quick glimpse behind the door. Eliot, Yeats and Larkin, the only representatives of the twentieth century are safely out of sight on the bottom shelf. Tiptoeing out of the study as if he is frightened of waking a light sleeper, Richard closes the door gently behind him and joins his mother in the kitchen.

When the kettle boils she rinses the pot out with water. Then she boils the kettle again, takes the tea leaves out of the Chinese tin he gave her and adds the water. He wants to be kind to her in the moments they have alone together but the anger gets in the way.

"Mum, I read the thing in the paper about Dad."
"They make me so angry that lot, snooping into other people's business."
"How did they get the photograph?"
"You missed ever such a lovely bonfire night Richard... everyone was there... you ought to bring Cathy down for it next year..."
"Mother did you give them the photograph?"
"What photograph?"
"You know, the one I took of Dad on his birthday, the one that used to be on top of the television."
"Oh yes, that Jackie Prescott woman must have taken it when she came down to research the book."
"And you let her take it?"
"No, I didn't notice it had gone until after she left."
"Have you asked her for it back?"
"I'm sure she'll bring it back with the other stuff."
"What other stuff?"
"The papers and things."

"You let them take Dad's papers?"
"I just left them in the study."
"How could you let them do that?"
"Well, you didn't want to know about it."

                *   *   *

Richard walks out of the house slamming the front door as he goes. At the end of the road he reaches the creek. The houses cling to the edge of the water like seats in an auditorium without a stage. Abandoned boats lie keeled over on the oozing mud. At low tide the air is heavy with the smell of seaweed and the cries of gulls. The creek was a vast wound he could never walk round as a child.

At the far side of the creek he enters the churchyard. As he shuts the gate he looks back. The sun reflected on the distant water makes the creek appear fuller. He feels he is etching the view on his memory – the way he used to look out of the rear window of his parents' car.

After the funeral he came down to sprinkle the ashes: a quiet farewell. He came down from London in the heavy snow. The roads were impassable; the train delayed. Even after death he kept his father waiting. The snow was cleared from the ground. The ashes fell from the scattering urn. Seeds from the hand of the sower – dark against the snow. Settling into the hard dark ground they disappeared as he stood with his head bowed, the tears pricking his eye-balls.

He walks out of the churchyard. Cathy is waiting for him. They walk on in silence through the gathering gloom. They never feel at ease walking in the city at night but here the giants and villains are images of childhood fears conjured by the rustling trees.

Richard runs ahead towards the water. He never walked all the way round the creek as a child. His mother worried about the tide cutting off their path. Nowadays he never runs further than the bus stop. He spits several times to remove the phlegm which collects at the back of his throat.

The moonlight reflects on the water making it seem fuller. Maybe it is a trick of the darkness. No there is definitely more water. The tide is in. Cathy catches up with him and slips her arm through his as they walk beside the dark creek. The water laps against the shore and the stars are bright in the clear night air. He clasps Cathy to him and they kiss.

*   *   *

When it is too dark to carry on working in the garden Dorothy comes indoors. In the kitchen the glistening worktops gleam at her. After her visits to the hospital she made do with cheese and toast. The meal is ready but Richard and Cathy are still "resting" before the meal. She does not like to disturb them.

For a quarter of a century she has cooked Henry's food. His desires have replaced her own; the cupboard is full of his favourite tins of soup and she no longer feels hungry. At last she can get rid of the tins. She selects a cardboard box from her horde under the stairs. There are so many cardboard boxes that there is not enough space for them all in the cupboard. To fit them in she stacks them folded, cutting the tape along the bottom and folding them flat. There are about twenty folded boxes in all. She selects a sturdy box – one that originally held whisky – so it must be good and strong. Taking the scissors from the rack and the tape from the cutlery drawer, she carefully reconstructs the box on the kitchen table. When it is complete she slots together the cardboard inserts which stop the bottles from rattling.

Nestling between the cardboard partitions, trying to be whisky bottles, the tins look so neat that she wishes they were going on a long journey. She will ask Richard to put them in the garage until she decides what to do with them. She can't go knocking on doors, saying "My husband's just died and here are some tins of soup which I bought for him." The Oxfam shop wouldn't want them. Perhaps Richard would like them or maybe the supermarket would agree to take them back. She should have checked the sell-by dates before packing them away.

Henry's last months had been an orgy of self-denial. No fat, no salt, no spices – no taste and no pleasure. Now that the soup tins are packed away she wonders what else she can discard. She chucks the salt substitute into the bin. Now that she has proper milk which the milkman delivers, she will be able to start collecting bottle tops for the guide dogs again. Richard used to argue with her about it. He said it was stupid to throw away cooking foil while she painstakingly washed the bottle tops and gave them to the guide dogs.

"Why don't you buy them a roll of foil, or just give them the money?

She is not giving money, or foil, or bottle-tops – she is giving herself. She gives a small part of herself to the guide-dogs for the blind — the rest she saves for her husband and her son. Only the collector for the guide dogs ever says thank you.

*   *   *

Cathy turns on the television and lies on the bed. His parents had bought the television for the soccer-mad teenager who had to watch *Match of the Day* every Saturday night. It is a long time since he has watched a black and white television. The BBC globe rotates calmly in the corner of the room.

> *"In tonight's programme we will be talking to Jackie Prescott, author of the forthcoming biography of Henry Dawson. In her book published tomorrow, Jackie looks at the off-screen life of the mysterious medievalist, whose love of literature brought pleasure to millions..."*

Richard reaches towards Cathy's body, warm beneath her crisp blouse. She rests her head against him. He moves her hair out of the way so that he can see the screen.

> *"... Jackie, in your book, you explain how Henry Dawson gave up the groves of academia for the bright lights of the television studio..."*

Moving his hand underneath Cathy's shirt he traces the ridges of her ribs. Very gently he moves up until he feels the outline of her breast. Her body tenses. He kisses her on the lips. She returns the kiss lightly without opening her mouth. He moves to kiss her again. Gently, so gently — with a light touch on his back, she indicates that he should pull away.

"Richard."
"Yes."
"Your mother said dinner would be ready about now."
"I'm sure we've got time for a quick *hors-d'oeuvre*".
"It doesn't seem right doing it here."

He moves his hand up Cathy's leg. Very slowly his fingers trace the outline of her thigh, feeling the smooth roundness as he searches for her moistness. Kissing her again, he forces his tongue into her mouth until she yields her body. Lying back she decides to let him do as he pleases. He works his tongue down her neck, coaxing her into a furtive enlimbment, bathed in the flickering beams from the screen.

When he finishes he cannot look her in the eye. He rolls off. He sees the photograph – gazing from the screen – watching him silently – the smiling face of his father stares out at him. Grainy skin, a smiling mouth that will never smile again – laughing eyes that can never cry.

Denise Neuhaus

THE CRISPENS

"The number to the theatre is by the telephone," said Mother, glancing at me in the mirror. I was lying on my stomach on the bed, feet in the air. She put on more lipstick, her mouth spread wide. Then she pressed her lips onto a folded Kleenex, leaving behind a dark pink kiss. I knew this was the way to put on lipstick. I had read about it in Seventeen Magazine. *Learning to put on lipstick takes patience and practice.*

My young womanhood with its endless evenings of practice loomed far away. I was only twelve; I could not wear lipstick. I jiggled my feet. What did people think about my mother when they saw her dressed up? Was she charming and cultivated? Did men admire her? Did they think that my father had a lovely wife? Maybe they could tell that she usually didn't wear make-up, that she went around in faded green cotton slacks and thong sandals. Maybe they thought, *Just somebody's wife. Somebody's old housewife. Somebody's old worn-out housewife trying to dress up and look good.*

My mother had once been young and beautiful; I had seen

photographs of her, with a full skirt and three-quarter length gloves and a hat like a plate. Her hair was golden brown. That was before she married my father and had us.

She had told my sister and me, in the casual and significant tone she used for such announcements, "The Crispens have invited me to the theatre next Saturday," and I knew she did not mean the movies. When she went out with the Crispens, it was always somewhere out of the ordinary. She was sitting on our orange vinyl sofa, crocheting. She crocheted endlessly, blankets which she called 'Afghans' and pillow covers, all of ugly colors, and all of which quickly turned dingy and stretched out of shape.

Her usual tone was threatening. *I am going to play bridge at Mrs. Ashland's this Saturday and if you kids smoke in this house or do ANYTHING I swear to God.*

She had never talked about the theatre before, but I knew that I was supposed to pretend that this was something she did all the time. I always tried to fulfil these silent demands. I could not bear to see her diminished, to suffer her haughty stare, her determined nonchalance, her raised eyebrows that would say, *And what is so remarkable about my going to the theatre* ? Her affectations embarrassed me; I wanted to protect her from the poverty of her life.

I said, "Oh," trying to sound slightly bored, but my sister was only six and as usual, didn't pick up the hint. "You mean to see a movie?"

I snorted contemptuously. "Dummy. The *theatre*. Not the movies. *God*, Lesley." She immediately started to sulk. Mother didn't look up from her crocheting and I pressed my advantage. "God," I said, disgusted by her hopeless ignorance, "don't you know anything?"

"Now, now," said Mother softly, as if appealing to my mature self who was compassionate toward the handicapped, the deficient, the backward of this world. She glanced at me conspiratorially: she and I knew what the theatre was; Lesley was just an ignorant kid. I shouldn't tease Lesley; she was just a stupid, ignorant kid.

Lesley began automatically to whine. Poor Lesley. She would always be literal-minded, obtuse, arrested in childhood. She would never learn the pretension of adults. She would never learn to drink coffee or alcohol or eat with her knife in her left hand or drop names without appearing to. She would never grow out of saying 'brung' instead of 'brought'. She would stay happily in the phases others outgrew, keeping her toy animals into high school, only to replace them with a collection of turtles, a tank of guppies, stray kittens. Her twenties she would spend working in a pet shop, cleaning animal cages. She would be offered promotions to the front part of the shop, and she would always refuse; she would be happy only when spared from having to talk to human beings.

She was still whining in the way we knew meant, *Tell me what I didn't understand. How am I supposed to know what you're talking about?* Mother interrupted her. She was going to have to rely on us kids to behave ourselves, she said. With our father overseas, and the theatre downtown, she would need to know that we could handle anything that came up. *Anything that came up.* What could possibly come up? Once Lesley had swallowed a penny. My mother called the doctor, but he said she didn't have to go to the hospital. In the summer, I sometimes stepped on a rusty nail or pulled an arm hastily through the barbed wire fence behind our house, and would run home, squeezing the split flesh until the beads of blood swelled and broke. I would have to get a tetanus shot at the doctor's.

These things could not happen so late at night. Lesley would go to bed, my brother and I would watch TV. Of course there were other, unspecified, possibilities: a fire, an obscene phone call, knocks on the door, burglars, *accidents*. These weren't, however, what she meant.

"I'm counting on you kids," she said. This was her generic warning, but I knew she was talking to me. I was always the one in trouble, and paradoxically, the one she assumed would be responsible if something happened, an accident, a fire. Already she had given up on my brother, who was too passive to get in trouble, except with me, or to do anything about it when it arose.

Lesley was still mad, her eyes small and hard, her breathing rapid and tense, her mouth opening and closing. She clinched her fists, ready to throw a tantrum. She hated being the baby, being the stupid one, the one who never understood. She always would, too. At sixteen, at twenty-five, at thirty, Lesley was still the same. During my visits home, we – Mother and I – would shake our heads and roll our eyes over Leslie's howlers and it would drive her mad. *God, Lesley!*

It was only much later that I felt ashamed and angry thinking of this, the damage my collaboration wrought.

We lived in the very last suburb. Behind our fence was a creek and then the barbed wire, and a field larger than our entire neighborhood with hundreds of cows grazing on it. Down the highway, past the houses, there were woods, and a lake, and the kids in the suburb built tree-forts there to hang out in and drink beer and smoke pot after school. We lived about an hour's drive from downtown and I had been there maybe three or four times in my entire life.

I spent the week trying to imagine what the theatre would be like. I had been to the ballet once, in elementary school, on a field trip. We went downtown in a school bus. The boys wore clip-on bow ties and the girls lace socks and patent leather shoes. On the end of each row sat a teacher or somebody's mother to chaperon us. They wouldn't let us get up at intermission. The stage was far away. One girl had a little pair of binoculars and showed off so much that everybody was whispering and trying to ask her for a turn and the teacher took them away.

I thought that the theatre would be small, chairs crowded intimately around the stage. Everything would be black. The set would be sparse. The play would be intellectual – something about ideas – with allusions to books that only cultured people would understand. My theatre was a sort of garret out of *La Boheme*, which my mother had seen with the Crispens, combined with the dark mystery of a night club. Because I thought of the Crispens as European, I elevated them from being merely rich and sophisticated; I made them bohemian.

Mrs. Crispen was not European but I would forget that. Getting married to Mr. Crispen had transformed her. I knew I was not supposed to mention anything about Mrs. Crispen's former life, and this was not difficult. She was a new being.

Mrs. Crispen's name used to be Mrs. Jackson; she had been our neighbor and she had had three children. She was divorced and a secretary, the only working woman anybody knew. All the neighbors talked about her and her children, who were never called in at dark, and were allowed to eat anything they wanted and stay up as late as they liked. She wore gold sandals and velour jumpsuits when she was at home. She both fascinated and frightened me. The word *divorcee* suggested a series of men, excessive drinking, parties; things as far from my mother's life as could be imagined.

Yet, my mother liked Mrs. Crispen and defended her to anyone who gossiped about her. When she married Mr. Crispen, Mrs. Crispen quit her job and sent her children to live with their father in Arizona.

Later, Mother would tell me that the children were sent to boarding school. This made me wildly envious; I imagined boarding school to be where girls learn to speak French and waltz and arrange flowers and give dinner parties. But Mother said it wasn't like that; it was a school for 'problem' children.

Mother only went out with the Crispens when my father was away. This seemed perfectly natural. My mother's other, stifled self belonged to the Crispens. Their charmed life was the one Mother would have led had she not married my father. I pictured her with some other man, who remained dim but generally resembled Mr. Crispen, driving around in the Crispens' Jaguar, to one art gallery after another, from a French restaurant to the opera.

Nobody drove foreign cars then, and I thought it daring. Foreign cars were considered slightly eccentric, almost effeminate, like soccer, imported beer, a man carrying a bag.

Why did I assume that my mother's true life was this? As she put perfume behind her ears and on her wrist, I rolled over on my back and read the instructions on the package of ultra-sheer stockings she had bought. They were supposed to be rolled on, not pulled.

She came over and held out her hand for the package. She was wearing a new bra with no straps and her old beige slip. Under the slip she had a girdle on. Even though she was as skinny as a rail, her stomach stuck out like a shelf from having children.

She sat down next to me and I watched her roll a stocking up each leg. As the stockings unrolled, the millions of tiny holes on her calves became invisible and her knees, which were really bony like mine, were pressed into smoothness. I knew her legs by heart: the needle-thin varicose veins behind one knee, which she got when she was pregnant, her faint birth mark, the pale mole on the back of her right thigh. She had dry skin and let me put lotion on her sometimes after her bath. I particularly liked to slather it all over the cracks in her heels, and watch it soak in, like dry, cracked ground filling with sudden rain.

She stepped into her dress and let me zip her. Then she picked up the black beaded bag she had had ever since I could remember and an embroidered shawl she had borrowed for the evening. She looked into the mirror a last time. She pulled on the curled tendrils of hair in front of each ear and patted the teased-up part on top.

I had watched her make her dress. I came home from school the day after she told us she was going to the theatre, and on the bed was a Vogue Original Design pattern and a folded square of black crepe de chine. I flung the material open, wrapped it around me and examined the pattern. I thought I would die if I did not someday have that dress. I was already taller than Mother, and larger boned, but just as thin and I knew it would make me look perfect.

It had no shoulders, but fell from the neck by a strip of rhinestones. It wrapped and twisted and had a slit in the back. It was a mini-dress and had cost $7.50 instead of the usual $1.95 because it was an original design.

I stared at the pattern envelope. I couldn't bring myself to open it and look at the instructions. I couldn't believe that dress could be cut out and sewn like a regular dress on my mother's Singer. It was a dress from a Paris boutique. English words could not describe that dress. I almost didn't want my mother to make it; I was afraid that she would ruin it, and I couldn't bear the disappointment.

I was taking Home Economics and Mother took me material shopping when I was to start a new project. I always left her at the broadcloth table and walked among the bolts of silk and satin. I loved the shiniest and brightest; the sheer, the swirling; taffeta, chiffon with sequins, dyed fur. Mother would come fetch me. *That's not very practical, dear. You can't machine wash silk. Don't you think that's an awfully large print for a skirt? Wouldn't you rather have dotted Swiss?*

I didn't want dotted Swiss. Or corduroy or broadcloth. Or a machine-washable skirt with a small flowered print. I wanted black and glitter and hot pink and a fake tiger-skin cape.

She would pull me over to the pattern counter. *I am NOT paying $5 a yard for something you can't even put in the washing machine for you to learn how to sew.* We would sit on the high stools, Mother flipping summarily through the pattern books. I would hardly be through the first section before she would be through every book they had.

She would urge me on. *You don't really want that empire waist, do you? I am NOT going to set those sleeves in for you.* But, I wouldn't be looking at the dress. I was looking at the way the whole picture made me feel: the way the model looked, and her hair and jewelry, the way she tossed her skirt and glanced over one shoulder. How did they look like that? Were they born that way? Mother would interrupt. *That is not appropriate for your age. Where on earth would you wear such a thing? Why are you looking in the designer section? Why are you looking at Vogue? You should be looking at Simplicity.* But I didn't want a pattern if I didn't like the picture.

Of course, Mother ruined the dress. First, she replaced the rhinestones with a strip of the material. Then, she lengthened it and closed the slit in the back. I hated it. I didn't know which alteration made me the angriest, but the dress was now a sickly relation of its cousin in the Paris boutique; it looked like something from the shopping mall.

And I was angry that Mother was all wrong for it, with her drooping arms and pointed elbows, her sloping shoulders. She hunched slightly, and the material that was supposed to flow down fell out from her body, making her look even more flat-chested than usual. Anybody could tell that she never knew what to wear, didn't know how to 'make the most of herself'. I hated her for thinking that she was being so daring to wear this dress, and for knowing and yet ignoring that it was all wrong, for trying without hope to be sexy and fashionable.

"You look pretty, Mom," I said.

"Thank you, dear," she said flatly. She was too used to being disappointed for it to bother her much.

We went out to the living room and she called my brother. His door opened and the whole hall was flooded with a smell like the boys' gym at school. He shuffled towards us and stood in the doorway to the living room, his head hanging, his hands in his pockets. He always looked as if he were waiting for somebody to step on him. His hair was long and greasy and over his mouth were some patchy dark hairs he thought was a moustache. He was going to have to shave and get a hair cut before our father got back if he didn't want to catch hell.

Mother looked at him a few seconds and then sighed, deciding not to say anything about his appearance. When our father wasn't around, she didn't like to disturb the peace. She said mechanically, "You can eat anything you want but clean up your mess. The number to the theatre is by the telephone. The Ashlands are at home if you need them. Lesley is to go to bed at nine. Yes, Lesley, at nine. Read her a story. One story. No, you may not stay up and watch television. I do not care if it is Saturday. Nine o'clock means nine o'clock."

She sighed again and opened the door. "Nancy, if you let any kids into this house —"

"We *won't* ," I said, exasperated. I had been through that with her about a million times that day.

She draped the shawl over one arm and took her car keys out of her bag. My brother was looking at the floor. I kept my eyes level with her thin shoulders.

We stood there for a minute. I could tell she wanted to say something else but couldn't think of anything to say. Finally, she said, "And no fighting."

I didn't bother to answer. My brother and I hadn't fought for over a year.

She stepped out onto the porch. I wished she would hurry up and go, but she stared at us as if she was trying to decipher through our blank faces what mischief we were plotting. She sighed, and finally, in the weary, slightly pleading voice she used when she was tired of being a parent and didn't really care any more what we did, said, "And *don't* burn the house down."

Now, this was an extraordinary statement. It was the first time she had admitted frankly that she could do nothing about our smoking; that however much she carped, and however much my father beat us, she knew the minute we were alone, we would light up. It meant, I know you're doing it; just don't let me find out.

My brother and I kept our faces completely expressionless at this new cynicism. As she closed the door, we both raised our eyebrows in amazement. We watched her start the car and pull out of the drive-way. Lesley ran off to the kitchen, but we waited, listening to the car drive down the street, and turn at the end of the block. We could just hear it continue towards the highway that would lead Mother to the city.

"Al*right!*" I yelled, going to the kitchen.

"Do you have a joint?" my brother called.

"Yeah, sure," I said sarcastically. "I have a whole pound."

Lesley was sitting at the kitchen counter, devouring a box of Oreos in the fashion she liked, which was to break them apart, and first lick the white middles out. I looked at her with disgust, ready to berate her for her childishness and the mess she was making, but she gave me such a fearful glance that I did not bother. I heard my brother putting on a record in his room, and I yelled, "The Stones!" I mixed myself a glass of chocolate milk. We no longer pilfered the liquor cabinet; my parents marked the levels on the bottles. After a moment, I heard Led Zeppelin at top volume.

My brother came back to the living room with his cigarettes and ashtray. We opened all the windows. I took one of his cigarettes and we both lit up.

Lesley said from the kitchen, "I'm going to tell."

"You do," I said, "and you're going to bed at nine." She resumed eating her Oreos calmly. "Is Mother's door closed?" I asked my brother. He was sitting on the back of the sofa next to the open window. He nodded.

I turned on the television with the sound down and then sat on the other end of the sofa and read the TV Guide while I smoked. "'Some Like it Hot'," I read between puffs. "With Marilyn Monroe, Tony Curtis and Jack Lemmon. 1959. Directed by Billy Wilder —" My brother ignored me, playing an invisible guitar to Led Zeppelin, with his cigarette hanging out of his mouth.

"Marilyn Monroe!" I said. "Don't you want to see Marilyn Monroe?"

"Who's Marilyn whatever?" said Lesley.

"God, Lesley," I said.

"Well, who is Mara-whatever?"

"Forget it. You're too little to understand."

"I am not."

"You are too. At eight o'clock. Don't you want to see Marilyn Monroe?"

My brother shrugged. "Sure."

"I am not too little."

"You are too. Shut up or you're going to bed at nine. I'm not even sure if you're old enough to see this movie."

Lesley started to whine, so I told her she could to shut her up. My brother still pretended that he didn't care whether he saw Marilyn Monroe or not, and I decided not to tease him about it.

It had been around my twelfth birthday that our cruel taunts, fist fights, and nasty tricks quite simply ceased, without fanfare or discussion. I had, in a few months, shot up nearly three inches, and was suddenly almost as tall as he; no longer was he so clearly my superior in a fight. I was about to go into the sixth grade and he, the seventh, junior high.

He had always been big for his age, and a bully; the kids at his elementary school were terrified of him. But in junior high, he wasn't the biggest around. There were older kids. And, it wasn't enough anymore to be just big. Strength was less important than the ability to run, to manoeuvre, to talk the right way, to carry yourself the right way, the way that said, *Don't fuck with me.*

My poor brother. He was lazy and actually a weakling. He could beat me Indian wrestling, but only just. He was flabby, uncoordinated and a slow runner.

The kids from sixth grade who went to junior high with my brother all seemed to spurt up and fill out that year. They spent the first part of seventh grade getting him back for all the they'd taken in elementary school. Then, they left him alone. He kept on eating and getting bigger and flabbier. He had acne. He never brushed his teeth, which were yellow and looked like a lab experiment. He took showers, but somehow always smelled, and his hair looked like it hadn't been washed in years. He had only one friend, a boy who avoided him, and girls ran from him in the hall at school.

My first year in junior high, kids would ask me, "Hey, is that weird guy in eighth grade *your* brother?"

He would marry a timid, neurotic and miserly girl who was terrified of strange inevitabilities, hoarding food, hiding money. She would keep him in a steady job and off drugs. My mother would be grateful, never say a word against the girl, count her blessings. My brother would be large and silent, moving crated washing machines and refrigerators from a factory floor into waiting trucks day after day, going home for lunch. He would lurch about, an enormous cripple; the men would leave him alone, not testing the strength of his bulk, speculating on the cause of his limp.

The news came on the television. While the anchorman mouthed in silence, Led Zeppelin shrieked in the background.

Then a reporter in front of the White House appeared and talked into a mike, his hair blowing in the wind. After a minute the camera cut to a man talking from a podium with the President's seal on it. We watched, smoking.

Some film clips were shown of soldiers in the jungle and then a map with arrows. I wondered idly how many planes crashed in Vietnam. A few a week? A day? I wondered what the chances were of getting shot down. I imagined a plane spiralling, then disappearing into velvety green, and a parachute bursting open, then floating down. How long would it take to notify the family? It might take weeks because of the jungle. Maybe they didn't tell the family right off, hoping they'd find the guy. Maybe they didn't even send out search parties for crashed planes. At least, they wouldn't if it crashed in enemy territory; it would be too dangerous. I wondered how much money the family got if the pilot was shot down and never found. Would it be enough to live on?

"How much money does the family get if your plane crashes and you're killed?"

My brother took a long drag. "Nothing that lucky ever happens to us." After a minute, he added, "Anyway, he doesn't fly a fighter plane. He wouldn't get shot down. He flies transport planes."

I knew my brother was right, but I still paused for a moment to imagine all of us in black, being photographed by the newspapers. I would be standing out in front, tragic and beautiful with a black veil and somebody would discover me and I would go to New York and become a model and make so much money that I could buy Mother anything she wanted and take her to the theatre and to French restaurants and go to Europe, just like the Crispens.

I had baby-sat for the Crispens once. Mother drove with me to their house, which was downtown and had an electronic iron gate. Inside, my first impression was that everything was in shades of white: the marbled hall, the two sofas, the numerous, stuffed chairs, the carpet. After a few minutes, I saw small, delicate wooden tables, Persian rugs. On the walls were paintings, of pink and blue nudes with enormous rears climbing into bathtubs. I held my mortified gaze stiffly from these, knowing I would blush if I looked at them.

Mrs. Crispen and my mother went upstairs, and her daughter, a girl of four or five called Anna Maria, came down shortly afterwards. She was wearing a pink pinafore. She had exquisite features, large eyes, white skin, glossy hair. We looked at one another, and our ages melted into insignificance; I saw us stripped to some fundamental sum of what we each had and did not have, of privilege, money, choices; the purity of *having*. Instinctively, I looked away until she had descended the stairs; I knew already that my defenses against females like her were small, essential, and had to be guarded closely, like a talisman.

Mr. Crispen followed his daughter down the stairs. He was not handsome, but he was elegant, and his face was sharply angled. He was so unlike any American man I had ever seen, he could have been of a different race. He was putting on gloves. I had never seen a man wear gloves before. He thanked me for staying with Anna Maria, as if I were doing him a great favor. Then he said, with a vague wave, in his strange, wonderful accent, "Please make yourself at home."

I never found out where he was from. When I could have asked, later, I did not. Swiss, Belgian, French? He had come over after the war. He had been orphaned. He was a DP, a Dispossessed Person, Mother had told me. I pictured a war-torn little boy with a Dutch hair-cut, in ripped lederhosen wandering past heaps of rubble, eating out of garbage cans, making his way to a port, stowing away on a ship, emerging onto the deck after days in the hull, the Statue of Liberty on the horizon.

He made his money in the construction boom, Mother had said.

They left, Anna Maria and I still facing one another. She examined me with a sort of benign curiosity, sensing inferiority and intimidation. Then, without a word, she went over to one of the white sofas and, with proprietary nonchalance, sat down and began to bounce up and down. I watched this and saw that she was at once establishing her right to do as she liked, and putting me at ease, telling me that the marvels she lived around were, after all, merely *things*. Things she used every day. Things I could use, too, for the moment. I watched her.

After a minute, she stopped bouncing and said, "We're not alone." I did not reply. "Cook's downstairs. She lives there." Then I saw that she was not only telling me that I was not in authority here, but also that I had been brought along merely to keep her company.

"Do you want me to read you a story?" I asked with icy politeness.

"No, thank you," she returned. "I will show you my room though if you like."

It was as large as our living room. In the middle was an enormous creamy lace canopy bed, and against one wall, a polished, heavy dressing table, covered with a lace ruffle. In her closet were rows of starched dresses with peter pan collars, bows, lace cuffs and below, dozens of shoes, each pair in a box.

But the best thing in the room was the mural, which covered one entire wall. It was of a little girl on a swing which was attached to the overhanging branch of a tree by ropes of woven flowers. Behind the girl was an enchanted forest with trees and birds and animals. The little girl was swinging out, her legs straight, toes pointed, hair streaming long behind her, dress billowing in the wind. I looked at it for several minutes before I realised that the painting was of her, Anna Maria.

That was when I knew that I would never be precious, to anybody.

"Some Like it Hot" started, so we turned off the music and

turned up the television. Marilyn Monroe looked drunk throughout the whole movie and slurred when she talked, but in a sexy way. It was hard to believe that she was, after all, only a female, of the same stuff as I. I thought she looked like an alien, or something that had been made up by special effects, like the idea of the perfect movie star.

The movie was very confusing. The men in the movie leered at her, as if they desired her and yet wanted to harm her. She was supposed to be the epitome of femininity, and yet she existed in opposition to every virtue women were supposed to have – modesty, chastity. Her near-nudity embarrassed me, not only because I knew it was immoral in the way *Playboy* was immoral, but because it was so acceptable. There seemed to be some special rule for Marilyn Monroe, which made it alright for her, but not normal women, to flaunt herself indecently.

We had a photograph of a woman who looked a lot like Marilyn Monroe. My brother had found it in a box in my parents' closet. When I was ten, I thought she *was* Marilyn Monroe. In the photograph, my father had his arm around her. They were at a party, somewhere overseas. (Europe, Asia; I never thought about it; he was just 'overseas'.) The woman wore a long dress, very low cut, and trimmed around the top with fur. Her shoulders and breasts looked as if they were perched on this bed of fur. Some people were standing around them in the photograph, holding drinks and laughing. My father was looking down the woman's cleavage with a stupid grin on his face.

During the commercials, we raided the refrigerator and made popcorn. Lesley fell asleep about nine o'clock, but when we tried to move her to bed, she woke up and made such a fuss that we left her on the floor in front of the television. At the end of the movie was the 'public service announcement', a voice which demanded reproachfully, "It is ten o'clock. Where are *your* children?" We always replied to this, "Out smoking and drinking and screwing around!"

I checked the TV Guide but the late movie did not interest me. I didn't feel like staying up, so I went to bed, leaving Lesley asleep on the floor and my brother smoking in front of the television.

This was the night my brother had the accident that gave him his limp.

Because of the accident, he would miss some school. He would begin to fail and eventually drop out. Then, he would start taking drugs in a serious way. One night, he would lurch down the middle of a major highway, against traffic, his pockets filled with pot, speed, LSD, waving his arms and shouting at the cars.

There would be a way to get a first offender's reprieve, which was to enlist. But the army would refuse to take my brother because of his leg, and he would go to jail for nine months. After jail, he would get married.

The accident happened like this:

From the middle of nowhere, I am jolted awake. The ceiling light jerks me up and then, immediately, my sister leaps screaming onto the bed. She jumps up and down on the bed and on me. I almost slap her, but then hear her disordered words: bathroom, shower door, glass, cut, blood. I push her aside and run out.

My brother lies on the tiled floor, propping himself up on an elbow. He is dressed. He looks up, calm, a little dazed, embarrassed, as if he knows something has happened, but he is not sure what. He is ineffectually wrapping a dirty bathtowel around his leg. Blood is spreading through the towel with steady progress.

The shower door is gone. Everywhere is glass, shattered into large and small pieces. Bright blood trickles down the cabinets and walls and on the toilet, and is all over the floor, mixed in with the glass. In the toilet is piss, my brother's urine.

My brother is wedged between the shower stall and the cabinet under the sink. The toilet is inches from his head. I have never realised before how small the bathroom is. He is wrapping the towel closer around his leg, looking at me confusedly. He seems to be waiting for me to do something.

"Let me see," I say, kneeling carefully in the glass. He smells and I blanch slightly. Then I lift the towel. The calf is sliced open to the bone in two bloody trenches, each about ten inches long. One starts near the knee, the other lower down, ending at the ankle. All around are more cuts, glittering with glass dust, the blood clotting and matting the hair on his legs.

Pure panic seizes me. I know I have gone pale and cannot move. I look at him to see if he understands how serious this really is, and he stares back at me dumbly. Then I realise, he is stoned. He would have to be stoned to have fallen back with such force through the shower door. I ask him what he has taken; he denies that he has taken anything. I think, *I will never get through this. I will not cope. He will bleed to death.* Here is the crisis Mother has always warned about. Here it is: an emergency. The middle of the night. Nobody at home. Nobody but me, and I have to do something. I freeze.

A moment passes. My brother watches me. "I'll get someone," I finally said, backing out of the bathroom. I see the bleeding again, swelling, engorging the towel and am afraid he will die while I am gone. I find some clean towels and make a kind of tourniquet. Then I run out.

I run out of the house in my nightgown and across the next door neighbors' wet lawn and drive-way to the Ashland's house. I ring the doorbell over and over again, without stopping, and bang on the door at the same time.

Mrs. Ashland, in her dressing gown, her head wrapped in toilet paper, comes to the door, listens, tells me to go back and wait, and calls to her husband as she shut the door. I obey, relieved to have directions to follow, to have an adult taking over, to have done what I should.

As I run back across the grass, I collide with my sister right in front of the next door neighbors' house. I shake her by the shoulders. "What the hell are you doing here?"

She begins to cry. "I was getting the neighbors."

I am livid with anger at her insubordination. "What do you think I was doing?"

I shake her harder.

"I don't know," she cries pathetically. I slap her. "You stupid idiot! Did you wake them up?"

"No!" She holds her face.

I push her down onto the grass and then yank her up by one arm. "Get in that house. You know Mother says they're trash. How dare you go to them? Don't you think I know what I'm doing?" I half-pull, half-drag her to the house. "Get in there and shut up. Do you want to wake up the whole neighborhood?"

I send her to bed and go back to my brother. He is holding the tourniquet, and now looking scared, like a wounded animal. I flush the toilet, replace the blood-soaked towels, help him sit up. We are both embarrassed now, by this intimacy, this touching; our indifference to one another has become our bond since we have quit fighting; we have passed from the fierce love and hate of childhood and into the mutual contempt of adolescents. We know this closeness is thrust upon us by sheer chance, as much as our sharing of the same parents. We know that we actually share nothing, except the desire to shed this present life; we know that we are already strangers who meet, touch, care only because of this present moment.

Mother has left her cotton housedress on her bed and her sandals on the floor, and I put these on. I glance at myself in the mirror. My face is white and my lips red. My hair is a mess and I pull Mother's brush through it a few times. I feel strangely excited.

Mr. Ashland comes and we carry my brother to the car and put him in the back seat. Then Mrs. Ashland comes and takes Lesley back to their house. I am afraid that she will try to make me stay behind as well, and am prepared to defend my right to go to the hospital, but neither object when I climb into the car.

I tell Mr. Ashland in an efficient voice the name of the nearest hospital and the theatre where my mother is. He nods without comment. When he turns in a different direction than the hospital, I say, "Hey, you're going the wrong way."

He says, "That hospital doesn't have an emergency room."

"Oh," I say. It dawns on me how limited my role actually is in this. After a minute, I add conversationally, "Well, wouldn't you just know. An accident just had to happen with my father overseas and my mother at the theatre." Mr. Ashland smiles a little at me but doesn't answer.

Mrs. Ashland has called the hospital to tell them we are coming, and when we drive up, there are two nurses waiting with a hospital bed on rollers. They don't seem very concerned, which shocks me. Even when they lift the bloody towels from my brother's leg and see the cuts, they chat cheerfully, like the school nurse used to when we would fall on the asphalt. I get madder and madder at this indifference, and am about to tell them that they'd better do something fast before my brother started to bleed to death, but then, he is gone, rolled away through some swinging doors. I follow and am left in the bright, dirty waiting room.

There are some children there, one with an ear-ache and one with a burn, not very bad, and some old people. After a few minutes, some policemen comes in with a man who is drunk, bleeding all over his head and yelling about his wife, calling her a bitch and saying he is going to kill her. The nurses, who march around like military sergeants, warn him that he will go straight to jail if he doesn't shut up. He tries to grab one of them, and she twists his arm so hard that he cries out and begins to whimper like a dog.

A Mexican comes in holding a cloth around his hand and he can't speak English and all the nurses are yelling at him at the top of their voices, trying to make him understand. The lady next to me asks me what was wrong with me and I tell her about my brother. She tells me that her husband had convulsions and she doesn't know whether it was epilepsy or a stroke.

Then I remember: what if he has taken some drugs? Should I tell them? Such a betrayal is nearly equal in import to the risk of his death. I stare at a nurse sitting behind the desk, writing. Then my mother walks in. She looks stiff and white. Her make-up lays on her face like a transparent mask. I can see the bags under her eyes that she had covered with a special make-up and her skin hangs down as if she is very tired. I try to say something to her, but she walks right past me and to the nurses' desk. I am dismayed. She isn't happy that I've done something right for a change, that I have handled an emergency. She has grimly assumed responsibility for this; I am now of no importance.

I watch her go through the swinging doors.

After a long time, she comes out again with Mr. Ashland. She stares at me for a minute as if she does not recognize me. She looks very small in her dress, as if I am looking at her at the end of a telescope. Her dress and make-up and teased-up hair stand out like a costume; underneath, she looks like she usually looks: tired and fed up.

She continues to stare at me and I wonder if it is that I am wearing her dress – she hates me to touch her things. Or, maybe it is that I have come to the hospital when I should have stayed at home. Or maybe she knows that my brother is stoned. Then I wonder, can she be in shock? That would have been the way a mother in the movies would act.

I briefly imagine Mother being paged at the theatre and then dramatically rushing into the hospital, her black dress in a swirl. Two gentle nurses would guide her to where her handsome son lies bleeding to death, and she would take his hand and gaze tenderly into his eyes.

She sighs, deciding not to mention whatever it is she is mad about. And, I know she had rushed over because that's what mothers have to do, even when their sons are smelly, have yellow teeth, take drugs. She is not in shock; she will take care of everything now.

She says, wearily, "Mr. Ashland will take you home."

When we drove up, the front door was open and all the lights were on. Standing inside were Mr. and Mrs. Crispen in their evening clothes. We walked in, and the Crispens and Mr. Ashland spent about ten minutes politely disagreeing about who should stay and clean up and wait for my mother. Finally, the Crispens won and Mr. Ashland left.

Mrs. Crispen said, taking off her gloves finger by finger, "Let's just see if we can't clean this up a little for your mother." Mr. Crispen followed her down the hall and I came last.

"Well!" said Mrs. Crispen, "When you kids have an accident you certainly know how to do it!" I laughed a little to be polite, and watched her. She was wearing a green taffeta dress, gathered at the waist and with a neckline like a heart. I wanted to see if she was really going to start cleaning up all that glass and blood in that dress.

Mr. Crispen surveyed the bathroom. He did not appear embarrassed; he seemed to be considering things.

"What we need is a bucket and some rags," said Mrs. Crispen with forced heartiness. I stood there, entranced. I had never been around the Crispens alone before. I wanted to study them.

Mrs. Crispen had changed from the days when she was Mrs. Jackson. She was blonder and thinner. I had heard Mother tell

Mrs. Ashland that she had had a boob-job and I tried to see if I could tell the difference. She had done it, Mother said, because they went to the South of France on vacation and the women there go topless on the beach. Mother had said this in an odd way, as though it were funny but kind of embarrassing and not very surprising. After all, she seemed to say, that's the Crispens.

The telephone rang and I went to answer it. Mother asked me where Lesley was, and I told her. Then I said, "The Crispens are here."

She groaned. "What are they doing?"

"We're cleaning up the glass," I said, even though nothing had been done yet.

"Oh God," groaned Mother. "Tell them to stop immediately."

"Mother says to stop immediately," I called to the hall.

Mrs. Crispen came and took the phone from me.

She said, "Virginia... Don't be silly... How is he? Well, thank heavens... No, no, don't worry... We won't... Of course not... You just do what you have to and... Alright... Yes... Bye-bye..." She put the telephone down. "Your poor mother."

Mr. Crispen had left the room and now returned with a bucket and some rags. He began to pick up the larger shards of glass and put them in the bucket. Mrs. Crispen bent down to help him.

Then she turned a little toward me, still bending over, to pick up a piece of glass that had flown out of the bathroom and onto the hall carpet. Her hair had fallen forward and across the side of her face, a perfect blonde curve, coming to a point on her cheek. Her neckline gaped open a little, and I could see the edges of her bra.

She said, "Well at least your brother waited til the end of the last act to have his accident!"

I didn't say anything.

"Your mother," she went on, "certainly enjoyed the show."
She looked up at me as she shook out the contents of the rag
into the bucket. I suddenly felt very tired and wanted them to
go. I knew that Mrs. Crispen felt sorry for my mother for being
married to my father and saddled with us while she was married
to rich, European Mr. Crispen. And I knew that there was
nothing I could do about that. I wanted to tell them that they
didn't have to clean up my brother's blood and the glass, that
I could take care of it myself, that I didn't need their help. But,
my part in all this was not to decide; I knew I would have to
wait until, eventually, they would leave.

When I was in high school, the Crispens got divorced. Mrs.
Crispen, my mother said, "came out of it very well." But a
year later, she found out that Mr. Crispen had hidden a lot of
money from her in Switzerland. When she tried to sue him for
some of it, the judge ruled against her.

When my mother warned me about the perils, the awful
responsibility, of adulthood, I knew already that the risks I
would undertake, and the damage I would live with, not only
from childhood, but collected at every stop ahead, would dis-
courage me, but not for long. I had already seen the women I
would never be.

The memory of Mrs. Crispen faded with her divorce, as
though she had again transformed. Into what? I never found
out. What I remember best from that night is not Mrs. Crispen,
nor her daughter, nor even my mother, who, like us children,
were only appendages, who could be discarded, ruined, protected as others saw fit. It is Mr. Crispen, the dispossessed
child who made dreams come true, who I remember best.

Mark Slater

VANISHING POINTS

"Are you sure you know where you're going?" Kate gazed up ahead to where the thin line of the sheep track vanished into the mist.

Richard wiped the moisture off his eyebrows. "We're off the map. The book says there's a footpath up ahead," he paused, running out of patience and confidence, "somewhere."

"Somewhere," Kate repeated, "Somewhere over the bloody rainbow."

Richard gave her an angry glance. Turning, he looked up to where Rachel was walking above them towards the dry stone wall that skirted the top of the valley. Her freckled face, with its soft cheeks and large brown eyes looked pale against the grey rock. It annoyed him that she should go off by herself with the mist coming down.

"Do you think we should call Rachel?"

"We?" Kate looked at him incredulously.

"She seems to think that the path is further up there."

"I know," Kate didn't seem to have much faith in either his or

Rachel's sense of direction. "You know she's hardly said a thing to me all morning."

Richard didn't answer. He began to clamber over a large pile of slippery boulders.

Stopping in front of them, Rachel turned and looked behind her. "Wouldn't it be more sensible to go back to where we lost the track?"

Leaning against a rock, he stabbed the soggy page of the guide book with his finger. "It says here there's a path up ahead. Why go all that way back?"

The sheep track they were on ran along the side of the steep slope leading up to the ridges. It was hard to follow and often, when it hit an outcrop of rock, disappeared completely.

Richard looked glumly up at the descending clouds. They were beginning to worry him, but turning back now would mean not being able to walk the ridge. If they got back on the path, even if it did get mistier, they could follow the small piles of cairn stones. He knew what he was doing. Kate was getting on his nerves, questioning everything he said.

The mist was coming down fast, it had already consumed the peaks up to their left. As he looked around he could see long, icy tongues licking the upper air of the valleys. Further down the mountainside, the monotonous roar of a waterfall could be heard, booming down its granite gulley. Below and behind that, Buttermere and Crummock Water, like giant puddles of solder, gave off a steel-grey light.

In five minutes the mist was on them; light at first, it grew rapidly thicker until it had wrapped them in an impenetrable whirling fog. Richard found himself suddenly alone and had to shout to judge the position of the others.

The world had shrunk around him, reducing his visibility to next to nothing. He looked around apprehensively. Cursing the mountain with its greasy outcrops of granite and the elemental treachery of the air, he leaned forward and crammed his foot awkwardly between two oily rocks. Nervously working the wet rock for a toe hold, his foot slipped and fear began to finger his intestines. Gulping a mouthful of fibrous air, he wedged his foot in and straightened his contorted body, steadying himself on an outstretched hand. He tried to remain calm, but his breath was coming in short staccato bursts.

Within the reeling mass of cloud he could find no fixed point against which he could locate himself. Shade upon writhing shade of white consumed the distance. He gripped the rock tightly. Turning his head to confront the billowing vastness, he searched for a momentary fissure, through which he could catch a glimpse of colour. Nothing. Nothing but the churning vertiginous floss, which made him dizzy with fear.

With every second that Richard stared, the invisible drop became more precipitous. As he felt the mountain tilting to topple him into the abyss, he slammed his eyes shut and swivelled around towards his sodden perch. Concentrating all his will, he fought for control of his body. His eyes still tightly shut he demanded and pleaded, but his stomach, flexing and pulling, wormed itself into a nauseous knot. His blood pumped panic to his veins. Shaking his head, he flicked the moisture off his hair and beard. His knees quivered against the denim of his jeans. Richard felt shamed by his inadequacy. Whenever he was denied visibility; when he could not define himself in relationship to something, he became nervous and confused.

Shaking his head again, he opened his eyes to find he was looking down on a dense green landscape. Thin tributaries of clear water gargled and raced around blacked-out forests and mountains stained with patches of orange and copper. In the middle, dwarfing the scene, Richard's white hand clasped its highest peak.

He looked away and focused on a small, ghostly tree, half consumed by mist on the edge of his vision. Scrambling towards it, his feet clumsily following his eyes, his heart began to slacken its tempo and his breath ceased tearing at his lungs. He stopped and listened to the milky silence. He could hear nothing but water; in the air and on the ground, dissolving everything in its cauldron of mutability.

Leaning back and forcing a note of confidence into his voice, he called out loudly to Kate. She answered irritably from close by. Surprised and reassured, he changed course in her direction. Cupping his hands he turned and shouted up the mountain, to where Rachel had climbed above the old dry stone wall.

"Rachel! For God's sake, please come down. We'd better stick together until this mist clears."

"Okay, I'm coming. Don't move."

Rachel sounded nervous and frightened. Against the background of the fog their voices betrayed them. Richard called out again.

"Kate!"

"I'm here!"

"Where?"

"Here. Behind you."

As Richard turned towards her a booming cacophany crashed through the air around them. He raised his arm instinctively as it rose in volume. Across from him Kate held her arm up in the same inadequate pose. He braced himself. They stood there frozen, until the last rock crashed to a standstill.

Kate's arm dropped. Not a single stone had bounced into their small, sighted clearing. She turned towards Richard, her eyes open wide.

Richard was already half way out of his rucksack. He flung it down and tore the map wallet from around his neck. Turning, he ran up the incline on all fours, scrabbling over the loose stones and slipping on the sodden moss.

"Rachel! Rachel!" He bellowed her name with such force that he spat phlegm from his throat into his mouth. "Rachel!" The scrambling and the shouting and the fear had already winded him. Gasping in the chalky air he fought against the pain in his ribcage. Pictures of Rachel formed in his mind, recollections of the last two days, vivid and dreamlike. Rachel lounging in the car beside him, the light burnishing her freckled arms; Rachel standing in the door of the cottage, the glow of the fire behind her; Rachel's eyes, pleading with him as they had done the night before. Each embryonic moment of memory gave birth to greater panic. To the fear that she would disappear; that the images would blur or recede; that she would vanish forever. Running and staggering he came to the dry stone wall. He fingered it momentarily, like a blind man, then turned and ran along it, leaping and falling over the broken stones at its base.

*   *   *

Richard noticed a pair of head-lamps flashing in his mirror and pulled into the middle lane.

Rachel looked up and peered sleepily after the disappearing car. "He's going fast."

Checking behind him, Richard eased the BMW back into the fast lane. The needle hit eighty. Above the quiet pulse of the engine the road hissed monotonously. Richard hated motorways. They were obviously efficient, but he always got the feeling he was being sucked down them; that he was no longer in control and was being driven as opposed to driving. His wrists ached slightly. The road was flat and he gazed ahead to the point where it intersected the horizon. He began to muse over the elevations he'd been drawing up for the hospital complex outside Brighton. The competition for the job was fierce. At least three big London partnerships. They'd have to meet all the specifications, come well within budget and think of more besides if they were going to get it. The whole office, junior and senior partners had been working flat out on it for the last month. Although he was owed a break, he felt uneasy about being away from the job.

Rachel slipped her feet out of her shoes and wriggled her toes. "This is nice." She stretched her tall thin freckled body, luxuriating in the afternoon sunlight that was falling in her half of the car. Richard adjusted his back in his seat. Rachel gave a little sigh of pleasure and turned to him. "Isn't it nice to be alone? Just the two of us. No worries."

Richard gave her a thin smile and tried to take his mind off work. He wanted to be alone with Rachel, but being alone with her was becoming more and more difficult. She leaned over and kissed his cheek, tugging at his neatly trimmed beard.

"So tell me a bit more about Kate?"

"Not much more to tell really. She did Textiles at college. Used to be a real raver. Still is from what I can gather. She's in fashion. I think she's a buyer."

"When did you last see her?"

"A couple of years ago at Joanna's wedding. That week-end you were working. Don't worry she's nice. You'll like her."

"Everything's nice isn't it." Richard arched his back; thought about apologizing, but didn't. The idea of someone else spending the week-end with them didn't appeal.

"Oh, I'm sorry, I still feel a bit dozy. She's great. Good fun. A bit nutty." Rachel paused. "Nutty but nice." She laughed.

Richard winced. "We'll be at the Keswick turn off soon. Have you got the address?" He pushed the speed up to eighty-five.

"Where did I put it?" Rachel began to rummage through her bag. After searching the dashboard and ferreting under her seat, she tipped the contents of the bag into her lap and began re-packing it. She lit a cigarette. "Where the hell is it. You haven't seen it have you?" Richard looked at her but didn't say anything. She swung around and unzipped her hold-all, pulling out some T-shirts and flicking through her sketch-books. "It's not here."

"It's in the back of the A to Z in the glove compartment."

"You sod. You knew all along." She sat back and withdrew into her cigarette.

Richard leaned back slightly in his seat. He shrugged his shoulders. "It was your responsibility. You booked the cottage. You took the details. I can't do everything for you." He leaned forwards and pressed a knob on the facia panel. Rachel's window wound down slightly. "I don't understand how you manage to lose everything."

"I didn't lose it."

"Can I have it then?"

"Get it yourself. You seem to know where everything is." Rachel glared into the middle distance and smouldered behind her cigarette.

Richard leant across. He could feel her contracting; moving infinitesimally but significantly away from him. Why, he thought, couldn't she have been a bit more organized about the week-end. It was her idea after all. He resented the fact that, even though he'd been busy, he'd had to pick up the food from the delicatessen on the way back from work. She hadn't prepared anything. Her laziness annoyed him. He took the A to Z out of the glove compartment and put it on the dashboard. Pushing the cassette in, and turning up the volume, he steered the car off the M6 towards Keswick.

"... *It's a thin line between love and hate.*
It's five o'clock in the morning,
And you're just getting in... "

Richard began to move to the music. He felt relieved to be off the motorway. As he changed into fourth and the car purred swiftly around the long curve of the slip road the weak sunlight began to warm his body. He could see no reason why Rachel should sulk. He'd put up with her sloppiness for years. He didn't consider it unreasonable to ask her to be a little more methodical in the way she approached things. He eased his wrists and tapped his fingers on the steering wheel.

"*... She opens up the door and lets you in,*
Never once asks 'Where have you been?'..."

Without looking Rachel stubbed her cigarette out in the ashtray. Glancing over Richard noticed it, it was piled high with butts and matches.

"*... All the time she's smiling,*
Never once raises her voice.
It's five o'clock in the morning,
You don't give it a second thought.
It's a thin line between love and hate ..."

Richard sang along to the chorus. After the boredom of the motorway he found the loud music invigorating. He remembered that he'd forgotten to contact the quantity surveyor and began thinking about the hospital planning applications he'd recently submitted. He'd have to phone the office from a pub. They were off the dual-carriageway now and the road had narrowed to single lanes. Along the roadside wooden fence stakes flashed by in a continuous blur.

Richard was reminding himself of the contents of the engineer's report when the road began to curve into a sharp bend. He felt the speed of the car dragging it out into the middle of the road, into the line of the oncoming traffic, braking hard he swung the car back in. There was a long, angry burst of a horn as a car, coming the opposite way, swerved to avoid them. Beside him there was a sharp, audible intake of breath. Richard's neck prickled. He cursed, "Stupid bastard!"

"*... It's a thin line between ...*" Rachel leant over and flicked the cassette player off. "That was stupid!"

Richard slowed down, but said nothing.

"You could have killed us then. You do realize, don't you,

that you're supposed to slow down when you get off the motorway, not go faster."

"He was cutting the corner, there was acres of space."

"You've been doing eighty since you left the motorway."

Richard made a supreme effort to stay calm. "I was merely going to say ..."

"You were going to blame that man. You've always got to be right haven't you!" Rachel paused, then continued, quietly but emphatically. "It was your fault!"

Richard kept his expression blank. He refused to allow her to wind him up. It was her usual tactic. If he said anything that upset her, she'd cause a scene. She knew he couldn't stand arguing, especially when he was tired.

"You've always got to prove your point! It's like that address. You always have to try to make me look stupid."

Richard concentrated on the driving. If she didn't shut up he was going to lose his temper.

"You set the whole thing up, didn't you?"

"I didn't."

Rachel's clenched hands shook in front of her. "God. You're pathetic!"

"Me!" Richard turned on her. "I wonder what else you've forgotten. Every bloody time we go anywhere, or do anything, you forget something." He was furious now. Furious with her and furious with himself for not remaining calm. He hated losing control.

Rachel lit another cigarette.

"You can clean out those ashtrays when we get to the cottage, they're disgusting."

She took a long draw on her cigarette and ignored him.

"You'd live in a pigsty if I wasn't around to clean up after you."

Rachel shouted at him. "It's your car. You brought it. You clean it up!" She stared in front of her. "You're always doing it."

"Doing what?"

"You're always talking to me as if I'm some bloody kid."

"Bullshit!" Richard jerked his head up and down angrily as he spoke. "I always know when you're talking bullshit. You always use the word 'always' all the time. You nit-pick and exaggerate, then accuse me of doing things I never do."

Rachel rolled her eyes upwards. She turned on him, her voice hard and accusing. "Let's face it. You never wanted to come on this week-end did you? You moaned about Kate. Even though she's an old friend of mine and I haven't seen her for years. You moaned about taking time off work. I bet that's all you've been thinking about all the way down the motorway, bloody buildings."

"That's not true." He contradicted her, but without conviction.

"You couldn't handle the idea of going away. Even on a week-end! You've got no sense of spontaneity."

"That's not true. I didn't mind."

"Then why've you been in a foul mood ever since we left London?"

"I haven't." He made his answer sound light, almost happy, but his mind was churning. Why did she always infuriate him? He thought hard about it. They were becoming blind to each other. They lived together, yet they existed apart. He hated the endless, futile antagonism of it.

As they drove on in silence he was glad of the twilight that fell around the car and between them. They'd been together for almost four years. Four years too long maybe. It was at times like this that he just wanted to wipe the board clean and start again. At the beginning, when everything had been simple and uncomplicated, he'd had a sense of her presence. A sense of her identifiable in her, 'otherness', he couldn't think of any other way of putting it. As the years had passed her presence had become vague. Despite their proximity, he could no longer see her clearly anymore. There was always something missing, or was it that there was something, some property of their relationship which had developed, which he couldn't see or understand?

The landscape outside had changed, dark craggy ridges elevated the horizon, accelerating the fading light. The road began to weave through steep, roughly cut valleys. Richard turned on the head-lights illuminating the mosaic of the dry stone walling that ran along the roadside. In the increasing darkness he began to sense, rather than see the mountains massing in the valleys.

Rachel leant down and picked the A to Z up off the floor by her feet. "Here's the address," she said softly. "Freshfield Cottage, Lodore, Borrowdale." Leaning over she rested her hand lightly on Richard's thigh. "Listen," she said, "I'm sorry."

Richard carried on driving and said nothing.

*   *   *

Outside the pool of light spilling from the kitchen window Richard paused, and turning off the torch, peered into the sea of darkness which had enveloped the cottage. He blinked, screwed up his eyes, decided he couldn't be bothered to carry on unpacking the car, and walked past it, scrunching down the long gravel drive towards the road. A dog barked in the distance.

The anger and resentment he'd felt in the car was turning into a mood of desperation. The sense of blindness he felt towards Rachel made him think of insubstantiality. If the relationship was insubstantial then was it wrong to continue it? But who was responsible for its being that way? Was it him?

Was it not so much something he couldn't see, as something he couldn't be? Richard chased his unresolved thoughts through his mind.

At first the sound of his feet and the dog were the only things audible in the still night air, but slowly, as his senses adjusted he became aware, despite his preoccupations, of another noise. He stopped to listen and the dog stopped barking. Richard concentrated hard on the sound, unable to define it. It seemed as intrinsic to the place as the coal black mountains that held the sky, like a canopy, above his head.

Looking back up the drive, searching for its source, he squinted into the darkness behind the cottage and caught sight of a thin shimmering line of light hanging from the sooty ridge. Following it down through the hatched shadows of the mountainside, Richard stared up at a waterfall. Within seconds it had disappeared. Blinking hard, he looked again, catching sight of it for a moment or two before it vanished. He thought of Rachel. She was like the waterfall, dissolving in the focus of his attention. Taking his eyes from the point where he had last seen it, he found he could only see the waterfall when he wasn't looking straight at it; when he saw it as part of everything else. He stared hard into the darkness, until his eyes became tired, then turned, crunching gravel underfoot, and looked down the valley to where Derwent Water glimmered behind a screen of trees.

In the foreground, amongst the walled fields, sinuous folds of granite had muscled their way to the surface, gleaming and sweating under the halogen light of the stars. Richard began to feel a sense of unease. He looked back up at the inky peaks that encircled the valley but could find nothing reassuring in their brutal forms.

Turning the torch back on, he played its powerful beam over several disinterested sheep and found himself becoming annoyed at the fact that Rachel always wanted to take her holidays in the bleakest, most God-forsaken corners of the world. The irritation and resentment of the car journey had not left him. Feeling tired and increasingly unwelcome he was turning to go back as the kitchen door flew open. It banged noisily against the coal bucket he'd left outside.

"Richard. Where are you?" Rachel was standing in the doorway, illuminated by the light. "Kate's going to be here in an hour. We've got to get everything sorted out and the meal ready before she arrives."

Richard waved the torch at her in reply. As he crunched back up the path he wondered whether the noise of the waterfall would keep him awake at night.

Richard stared at the pile of boxes on the floor, awaiting instructions. He'd unpacked the car and put everything else away, but he wasn't sure what to do with Rachel's painting things. Reluctant to speak he waited for her attention. When she finally looked up from unpacking the bags from the delicatessen, Richard was staring, absent-mindedly into the fire he'd lit earlier on. The low ceiling added to his height. As the light from the coal played over his face, softening his features and darkening his hair and beard, he looked younger; gawky and self-conscious. He jumped slightly when she spoke.

"Darling, will you take my drawing stuff upstairs into the bedroom. Could you sort out some wine?"

Tired and confused, but relieved to have at last received directions, Richard stacked the boxes under one arm, opened the door leading to the small cottage staircase, picked up the drawing board and pads and carried them up the stairs. Getting the board around the sharp twist at the top of the staircase proved difficult and he banged it loudly against the wood panelling.

"Be careful with it will you." Rachel's voice drifted up from downstairs.

Richard carried it all through into the bedroom and dropped

the boxes onto the floor. As he drew the folders out from under his arm, a pad slipped from his grip and fell open. Two bright, abstract compositions clashed with the faded paisley of the carpet. Richard looked at them. He turned the pad to face him with his toe. The pictures looked familiar. Kneeling down, he read, 'Wallflowers', in the corner of each page. He remembered the previous year, Rachel had discovered a small plot of them. The pictures reminded him strongly of the feeling of that early summer, but he couldn't pick out a single detail in them that looked anything like a wallflower. Rachel, he knew was good at recording feelings, but he found it strange that such a confused blur of colour could have such a powerful affect on him. He stared down at the pictures for a while then flipped the pad closed and went back downstairs.

The kitchen was suffused in orange light. Rachel had finished laying the table and had lit a number of small candles which flickered as the open grate fire on the old range crackled and flared. The room looked friendly and inviting. She looked up as Richard came in, tucking her hair behind one ear with her hand. Her soft, brown eyes smiled at him and he stopped, standing awkwardly in the low door frame. They looked at each other across the room.

"Please," she said, "let's not quarrel." Then more brightly. "Wine?"

Richard looked down at the fire. "It's still in the car. I'll get some more coal."

As he made for the door Rachel came across and blocked his way. She took his hands and drew them behind her back. Leaning against him she rested her head on his shoulder. Richard tried to remain distant, but despite himself, his body responded to her warmth.

"Please, it's so silly," she whispered, hugging him. "Let's be friends. I'm sorry about the car and everything. I know you've been working hard. I didn't mean to upset you. Let's just relax and enjoy the week-end. Can we?" She looked up and kissed him on the lips, "Please?".

Richard lifted a hand to his head and massaged his temples.

"You're tired, aren't you?" She ran a finger down his cheek.

"Yes, a little." An excuse had been found for him. In the nick of time a loop-hole had been discovered. Kate was about to arrive. He had to be placated. His anger and confusion mingled uncomfortably in the physical pleasure of their embrace. The closer he held her to him the greater the distance became between them. He became frightened of looking into her eyes, worried that she would see the desperation in his own. Rachel began to rub her belly against his and he drew away.

"I'll get the wine."

"Okay. Do you know where those cigarettes are I bought?"

"They're in the side pocket."

"Could you get them?"

*   *   *

As Richard closed the door and picked up the coal bucket he noticed a pair of headlights moving towards them down the valley. He collected Rachel's cigarettes from the car and remembering the brimming ashtrays took them out and cleaned them. He'd almost finished filling the bucket in the coal shed when the lights from the car clipped the windows. He put the shovel down and peered out through the window as a Volkswagen pulled up outside. He should have gone out and welcomed her but he felt too much resentment at her arrival to be hospitable.

He watched as Kate got out and stretched. As she twisted her head from side to side her hair bobbed over two large pendulous earrings. Her face looked over-exposed in the darkness. With its pointed chin and high cheek bones it seemed a little pinched. When she turned towards the car, the light from its interior revealed carefully made-up features. He watched as she looked around briefly, tugged her suede jacket around her small frame and began to pick her way through the darkness towards the front door. She was wearing a tight short skirt. He raised his eyebrows and picked up the shovel.

"Rachel, Rach, it's me-ee!"

Richard finished filling the bucket, picked up the bottles of Chablis from the car and walked back to the kitchen. Shrieks of laughter were coming from inside. He wiped his feet, closed the door and put the coal down. Kate and Rachel, oblivious to him, were lost in raucous, animated conversation.

"You look great!" Kate's voice was excited and shrill.

They both laughed, as Rachel, her hands on her hips, pirouetted unsteadily. Richard caught sight of white, but crooked teeth behind Kate's glossy lips.

Rachel came to a standstill. "You're looking good too. What style!"

"Thanks kid. It's the job. You can't sell fashion in rainwear and wellies." They both laughed. "Don't worry I've got my Kagool! I didn't have time to change. Two hours from Leeds to Keswick. Must be a record! There are some arseholes on the road."

Richard pushed the coal bucket over the concrete floor. It grated harshly. The two women looked around.

"Oh darling, I'm sorry. Kate this is …"

"The creature from the wood shed!" Kate laughed as she turned towards him.

Richard juggled the bottles of Chablis to get a hand free. "Pardon?"

"I saw you when I arrived."

He shook hands. "Oh!" Kate glanced at Rachel. "It is

Richard isn't it?"

They laughed as he answered, "Yes." He felt irritated at being made fun of. "I was getting some coal," he said, uncomfortably. Then to cover his embarrassment: "How about a glass of wine?"

"Now you're talking." Kate looked around. "It's great this in't it?" She flopped down into one of the armchairs by the fire. Slipping her shoes off she massaged her feet with her hands. "It's so dinky. I thought it'd be somewhere really posh."

Richard was taking the cork out of the bottle. "Why's that?"

Rachel sat down by the fire.

"I don't know. I thought as you were an architect."

"Actually, it was Rachel's idea; to come here." He passed over the drinks.

"Oh, I see!" The two women laughed. Kate took a sip of wine. "Oh! this is nice. What's this?"

"Chablis, sorry I didn't have time to chill it." Richard apoligized.

"Chablis. Nice!" Kate smacked her lips, inspected the glass against the firelight and added regally. "Very, very nice!" She chinked glasses with them. "Cheers! Well go on then! Chink!" Rachel chinked her glass against Richards. "Here's to us!"

Richard sat on the floor in silence, occasionally poking the fire. As the two women discussed mutual friends and acquaintances he mulled over the project at work, organizing himself for the coming week. He re-filled the glasses, vaguely aware that he was drinking too quickly.

As the conversation progressed his thoughts turned back to Rachel and he began to feel irritable. The compromise he felt she'd forced him into increased his resentment. When she looked over at him he didn't look back, but occupied himself, staring at the fire, or reading and re-reading the label on the wine bottle. She'd made him look inadequate and boring in front of Kate. As he topped up the glasses he studied Kate's face. She was laughing again, throwing her hand up to her mouth. She acknowledged him for a second, then turned back to Rachel.

"So how's work?"

"Couple of exhibitions. Sold some paintings."

"Great. How many?"

"Ten this year. I've got an agent now who... Are you alright?" Kate had screwed up the right hand side of her face and was rubbing her eye. "S'alright. Contact lenses. It's the fire."

The timer on the cooker began to rattle and ping intermittently.

"I'll do it." Pleased to have something to do, Richard got up slowly from off the floor. The wine had made him feel groggy and tired.

Out of her left eye, Kate watched him uncoiling his long legs as he stood up. "Bloody 'ell. You never end, do you?"

"What's it like wearing contacts?" Rachel asked.

Kate stretched her jaw and blinked, trying to work some moisture into her eye. "Why, you thinking of getting some?"

As Richard opened the oven, the small pots of lasagne seethed and bubbled on the shelf. "That's why she paints abstracts. She's as blind as a bat."

Kate laughed.

"Shall we eat?" he said.

During the meal, Richard found that though he had to suffer a certain amount of small-talk, the conversation had at last begun to take him into its orbit. The wine, which he'd drunk about a bottle of, was beginning to effect on him. Trying to remember what it was he'd felt so bad about earlier on he found himself losing the thread of his thoughts. He still felt distant from Rachel and cheated by her, but the wine had clouded his mind and, for once, he was pleased it had.

When they'd finished eating he opened the third bottle of

wine. Feeling a little more sociable he re-filled the glasses, spilling some drops onto the table cloth. Kate's initial rudeness, he decided magnanimously, could be put down to nerves, and the kind of sarcasm that people used when they felt they needed to assert themselves; she really wasn't that bad. Pleased to have a new audience, he told some of his architect's stories. Even Rachel laughed, which made a change from her usual, tight-lipped smile.

The irritation that he'd felt by the fire began to lift. Although he was still angry with Rachel he began to find a welcome distraction in Kate's gregariousness. Having finished one of his party pieces, he relaxed and listened absentmindedly to the womens' conversation, turning the base of his wine glass on the table with his fingers, as if he was tuning a radio.

"Cannes. What's it like? I've always wanted to go to the South of France." Rachel's voice emanated from the seat to his right.

"What d'you wanna go there for?"

Richard looked up. "Because she's so sophisticated. Hadn't you noticed?" He was planning on saying something else but Rachel cut him short.

"It's the light. Have you seen any of Kubin's work. Or Klee's? Remember that print we've got at home – " she turned to Richard, " – in the hall. The Klee. Those colours that seem to just shimmer in the air as if they don't actually belong to anything. Beautiful."

Kate nodded in agreement. Richard turned his head unsteadily and looked at Rachel properly for the first time that evening. Her eyes were pleading with him in the same way they had before Kate arrived. Her slender fingers were holding her wine glass too tightly. He could see the white, translucent skin around her finger tips. She turned from him when Kate spoke.

"What are you working on at the moment?"

"Well I'm looking at a lot of Degas, especially his later

work."

"Degas, that's old stuff in't it? Didn't he do all the ballet dancers?"

"Yes, he went blind towards the end of his life, and his work becomes more abstract. I think there's far more emotion in his last paintings than in anything else he ever did."

"Yeah, I know what you mean." Kate was listening attentively.

"Lots of painters who've worked in the South of France have got that same feeling for colour." She turned to Richard. "I'd love to go down there to work. It would be gorgeous. We could go to Ronchamps." Her hand slid over onto his thigh. "You've always wanted to."

"Ronchamps?" echoed Kate, quizzically.

"Le Corbusier."

"Architect." said Richard.

Kate looked at them both and smiled. "That'd be nice."

The grip on his leg tightened and then relaxed. Richard, although he was beginning to feel a little drunk, felt the pulse of tension earthing itself in the flesh of his thigh. He looked back at Kate.

"Did you do Fine Art?"

"No, Textiles. Only the clever ones did Fine Art!"

"Oh Kate, that's not true!"

"Actually, the real reason was," she leant across the table towards Richard, confidentially, "they didn't trust me with the fellas. I'm alright with 'em when they've got a few clothes on, but when they take 'em all off..." She rolled her eyes. "I'm uncontrollable!"

Richard laughed loudly.

"It was always Kate's department that had the best parties."

"So you had all the fun, whilst the boring ones went to life drawing classes." Richard felt Rachel's hand slip from his leg. "What did you say you were doing in Cannes?"

"A show. I was buying for Roncali's."

Deciding that he was lagging behind in the conversation Richard tried to sound knowledgeable about the fashion world. "Aren't they Italian?"

Kate hooted with laughter. "They're a trade retailers in London. Ron and Carlene Coleman."

"So, what were they doing there?" Feeling slightly embarrassed he picked up his wine glass and had another drink. He waited for a reply; none was forthcoming. "I mean they don't sound like the sort of people you'd find in Cannes."

"That's fashion!" A broad smile spread across Kate's face as she shrugged her shoulders dismissively. "Cannes is full of people pretending to be what they're not."

Richard felt that her smile, after it slid away from his face, had become a different expression by the time it reached Rachel's. But he couldn't decide what sort of expression. "More wine?" he said lifting the bottle off the table.

Kate pushed her glass over. "Now, if you want to see real style, you've got to get as far away from a clothes shop as possible."

*   *   *

The coal had burnt down to a brittle, orange crust. It gave off a quiet, consistent glow, less agitated than the dancing light of earlier in the evening. The candles had burnt down and the room smelt of coffee, cigarettes and wax. Across the table and directly between him and the old range, Kate, her blond hair circled by the halo of the fire, was talking about Peru. Richard, mesmerized by her rolling Yorkshire accent, watched her animated face as it acted out the story she was telling. The coffee cup he was holding hung at an angle to his fingers. Occasionally he would focus on a place name or an expansive gesture only to slip back afterwards into his own eddying thoughts. He struggled to harness them, wondering what it was about Kate that made her so attractive. There was something about her that he felt he could relate to. She wasn't beautiful. Not beautiful like the perfect faces of women in the old masters; serene in their expressionlessness. The word expressionlessness, like some articulated garment in a washing machine, tumbled around his brain. He blinked. The thing about Kate, he decided, was that she never stopped expressing herself. Trying to imagine what she would look like at rest; asleep or dreaming, all he could see were the constantly migrating features of her face. He took another sip of coffee, put the cup down and yawned.

"We're not boring you, are we?" Kate enquired.

"No, no, not at all."

"He's tired, all that driving." Rachel's interjection annoyed him and he was about to frown, when Kate put her head on one side and looked at him sympathetically.

Richard smiled, a tired, but tolerant smile, and watched Kate as she leaned back, on her chair towards the fire. Stretching her arms out, she let her head drop onto the back of her shoulders. Starting with her neck, he began to explore the shape of her body. When she pulled herself forward, Richard felt her eyes on his. He looked up, expecting to meet a disdainful glare, but Kate's eyes neither said, nor acknowledged anything. Instead they turned away from his.

"So what fabulous walk are we going on tomorrow?"

Rachel took her cigarette from her mouth. Her voice sounded tired. "Depends on the weather. I'd like to do Buttermere Ridge. Tomorrow's the only day we can do it." The words seemed to retreat from her mouth, rather than advance. Richard looked at her, but found he couldn't focus. "Maybe I'll do some work on Sunday." She stopped and started to twist the glowing butt of her cigarette against the side of the ashtray.

He said nothing, although he knew what she wanted him to do; he felt incapable of even the smallest gesture. The sense of desperation he'd felt earlier on that evening welled up inside him again with a renewed force that cleared the alcohol from his mind, leaving him feeling cold and momentarily lucid. He shivered. In the short silence that followed he heard distinctly, for the first time that evening, the sound of the waterfall.

Kate broke the silence. "Have I been jabbering on or what? You two look whacked. How long's this walk gonna take?"

Rachel ran a hand through her hair and yawned. "About six hours."

"Six hours! The clocks have just gone back. It'll be dark by half past five. Come on you two; bed, or you'll never get up in the morning." Pushing her chair back and ignoring Rachel's protestations, Kate got up and began clearing the table. Rachel got up and resting a hand on the high mantlepiece, close to the ceiling, stared down at the brittle shell of molten coal in the range. Richard finished the last of the wine. Rachel looked over to Kate.

"I'll do that. Why don't you get your stuff in. Richard will give you a hand."

Kate put some plates in the sink, "Okay."

Richard got unsteadily to his feet, then remembering the torch, picked it up and went out after Kate. He shone it from the cottage out to her car. She was standing with her back to him, bending slightly at the knees and hips, rummaging about in the boot. He followed the black stockinged legs, up in a question mark, to where her blouse hung loosely in front of her. He watched her as she tugged out a suitcase and thought how pretty she looked. He tried to imagine the two of them together. 'Richard and Kate,' he thought; it sounded far better than 'Richard and Rachel.' He'd always felt they'd cancelled each other out; the two 'r's. Whereas 'Kate'; 'Kate' sounded really good. An overwhelming desire to put his hand on Kate's backside drew him towards her. There was no plan of seduction in Richard's mind, as he steadied himself to walk over to the car.

"You look nice." He said.

The question mark turned into an exclamation mark as Kate stood up. "What did you say?"

As she turned around to face him he put his arm behind her and pushed her, with his body, back against the car. A few confused seconds followed whilst Richard attempted to kiss her on the neck and Kate found something to brace herself against. She gave him a push. Richard stepped back. In a fluster of embarrassment he stared at the ground.

"What did you say?" Kate repeated incredulously. There might have been the slightest hint of curiosity in her voice, but Richard was too drunk to notice it.

He spoke to her knee caps. "You look nice." His eyes had reached the level of her hips when she began to laugh. Quietly at first, then it began to burst out from underneath her hand which she clamped over her mouth. At a complete loss for what to do, Richard began to laugh as well. It seemed to ease the tension. Still laughing, Kate turned him round by the shoulder and shoved a suitcase in his hand. A light went on in the bedroom window of the cottage. She pushed him towards the kitchen door.

"Get inside."

When they got back into the cottage, Rachel had cleared the table and gone up to bed. Richard stood, swaying ridiculously, in the middle of the room, he was now completely unsure of what he was doing. Kate took the suitcase out of his hand and steered him towards the staircase door.

"Go to bed, piss-head."

He could still hear her laughter as he groped his way up to the bedroom.

The old ledged and braced door creaked loudly as he ducked into the low bedroom. Closing it left him in complete darkness; a deep whirling darkness that clung to the skin and smelled of moss. Keeping one hand on the handle he waved the other around his knees, checking for obstructions, like a bather entering cold water. Reassured, he edged his way towards the bed, the sharp rake on the floor making what little sense of balance he had left, virtually useless. Reaching the bed he sat down and tried to take in what had happened downstairs. The shadowy outlines of the room scrolled up and down maddeningly in front of him. The scene with Kate had upset him not so much because of what he did, but because he did it without thinking. He tugged at his shoelaces.

"What were you laughing at outside?" Rachel turned, pulling the covers over her head.

"Just a joke."

Richard got undressed and slid quickly into bed. Lying still for a minute he listened to the distant pounding of the waterfall. Closing his eyes he found himself thinking about Kate. Whilst his body began to warm in the bed, his drunken imagination began to re-enact the drama of the failed seduction. He turned and put his hand on Rachel's warm backside kneading the skin, slowly and softly beneath his fingers.

The flesh tensed as Rachel arched her body slightly away from him. "Your hands are cold."

Thinking of the point where Kate's black stockings disappeared into the darkness of her short skirt, he pulled her body towards him and began delicately to trace the seam with his fingertips, down the back of her thigh.

Rachel flinched. "Tickles," she said, and squirmed slightly.

Kate leaned against the wall and rested her head on her arm, her mouth fell open and her body twitched as he began to ride the skirt back up her thighs.

"What are you doing?" Rachel turned, as Kate turned, and

took him in her arms. Her small, compact body responded perfectly to his as he lifted her up, against the wall. Within the broken, half-lit moments that followed; as his desires were translated into a flickering stream of images, Richard gorged himself on every detail of Kate's body. It was tantalizingly complete. He pushed, and pulled her in towards him.

"Don't, don't squeeze me so hard."

He looked at Kate's face but it had become expressionless. Her face had become the face of a woman asleep. She fell away from him, turning slowly, her body growing smaller and smaller. As she kicked and writhed, squirmed and shuddered, she looked like she was making love to a ghost.

Richard opened his eyes. His face was pressed up against Rachel's breast. One eye was buried in darkness. With the other, he looked around. He could see nothing but shadows and flesh. Moist, oily skin moved beneath him. The smell of warm, sweet sweat filled his nostrils. He groped around, lost in its vastness. Far away he heard someone laughing.

"What are you doing?" Rachel pulled him up towards her. "Are you alright?"

Staring along Rachel's shoulder, which ran like a ridge, out into the darkness, he felt his body becoming heavy and unresponsive. "Tired." he mumbled. Down below in the dampness of the bed, he could feel his erection shrinking and slipping out from between her legs.

Beneath him, Rachel's body had become as hard as stone. "Get off me. You're so bloody heavy." Her voice was full of contempt as she pushed him aside and wriggled out from underneath him.

Slumped on his side of the bed, Richard closed his eyes and begged silently for the refuge of sleep. His path into oblivion, when it came, was a humiliating one. At first below, then rising above the sound of the waterfall outside, he could hear the murmurs of Rachel's climax; beyond that, deep in the stillness of the night, there was another sound, the sound of a woman's voice, raised in laughter.

*   *   *

"Rachel!" Richard screamed, and clambered onto the fallen stones, pushing and sweeping at the mist with his arms. Then, in the gruesome realization that he might be crushing her body beneath his weight, he scrambled off and ran frantically around the area, craning his neck, peering forward, then rushing into the fog. As he hurled himself at the mist, groping blindly around him, images of Rachel, almost tangible in their clarity, cascaded through his mind in a vivid torrent. He saw her profile, as he had only minutes before, milky and white against the dry stone wall. It was the last time he'd looked at her. Panicking at the thought that it might dissolve and leave nothing behind it, he fixed the picture in his mind with all his remaining strength. Leaping and stumbling he reached the bottom of the fall and bellowed her name. Then coming to a sudden halt, he stopped and stared at a shape in the mist. He blinked and shook his head, momentarily unsure that what he saw wasn't another memory thrown clear of his racing thoughts.

Rachel, her hands clasped around her ears, was sitting amongst a pile of stones, rocking silently backwards and for- wards. Kneeling beside her, afraid that what he saw might disappear in front of his eyes, Richard held out a cautious arm and touched her shoulder.

"Darling, are you alright?"

"I broke the wall," she said without looking up.

Richard looked at her face and hands, she was badly bruised but there was no blood except for a little oozing out from underneath two broken fingernails. "You haven't broken anything?"

Rachel took her hands away from her ears. "I broke the wall." She looked at her hands then up at Richard. "It's stopped," she said. He put his arms around her as she leaned against him.

Richard pulled her more closely to him. The fear that had been pumping through his body had evaporated in his relief at finding her alive and the sense of desperation that had been haunting him for days dissolved as he cradled her in his arms. She was with him once again; entire and complete. He sensed what it must be like for a blind man to have his vision restored. Feeling her warm breath on his arm, he looked down at Rachel's slightly bruised face. Kissing her forehead, he felt he could have sat on the mountainside holding her forever.

"You must tell Kate to go," her voice was as anonymous as the mist.

Richard sensed the spell of their reunion had been broken. "Yes, yes, of course. Don't worry, it's alright." He tried to eradicate any sense of uneasiness from his voice.

Rachel looked up at the pile of stones stretching away like a causeway into the fog. "I feel so bad about the wall."

Kate's worried voice drifted up through the mist. "Is she okay?"

"Yes! She's a bit stunned."

There was a relieved silence; then Kate's voice again. "We'd better go back."

"Yes, we'll come down." Supporting her with his shoulder Richard lifted Rachel up and swung her arm behind his neck. Together they began picking their way down the slope. Rachel turned to stare back once or twice at the broken wall. He shouted into the fog to Kate, "Head back to the gill. We can follow the sound of it down to the waterfall."

Neither Kate nor he dared to speak as, in increasing desperation they followed each others hunches and one direction after the other was tried in vain. In some places the landscape was thickly clotted with fog and in others patchy and sparse, but nowhere was any sound or place within it identifiable. Richard's heart was once again beginning to thud against his chest when Kate picked up, through the mist, the thin pulse of water trickling down the mountainside. They stood motionless, listening hard, not wanting to lose a syllable of its distant, elusive sound. Then, agreeing on a direction by pointing and shaking heads, they staggered and clambered towards it.

Within minutes they'd reached it, and following it down, dropped out of the sky into the visible world. Richard, looking up behind him at the cloud layer, gave a long sigh of relief and Kate smiled, but little else was said as they made their way down towards the deep gulley of the waterfall. Richard supported Rachel, and together with Kate, helped her to climb down the more precipitous drops of rock. The vertigo he'd felt on the mountainside in the mist no longer affected him and his confidence began to return. He feasted his eyes on the clearly defined lines of the landscape around him; the sharp ridges running down from all sides into the valley and the glassy contours of the two lakes at the bottom.

As they worked together carrying Rachel, Richard could feel Kate was uneasy. Her help and sympathy evoked little response from Rachel, who, although still shocked was slowly beginning to come round. He realized he was going to have to ask Kate to go; and he was growing anxious as to how much Rachel knew. His happiness that the crumbling structure of their relationship had been reconstructed was marred by the conspiracy between the two of them, against Kate, which made him feel wretched and guilty. As they picked their way carefully down the mountainside, further below them in the gulley, the deep booming voice of the waterfall was becoming increasingly audible.

Before they set off back to the cottage, Kate took the first aid kit from the boot of the car and put plasters on Rachel's cut fingers. Whilst they were driving she took the blanket off the back seat and put it around her shoulders. Richard busied himself, fiddling with the hot air vents, testing them with his hand and directing them towards her. Wanting to know exactly what had happened, he plagued Rachel with questions, to which she gave only the briefest answers. Kate eventually leaned forward and putting her hand on Rachel's shoulder, insisted that he stopped pestering her. Disappointed, but assuming she still felt slightly stunned, Richard stopped.

For most of the journey Kate sat in silence on the back seat occasionally leaning forward to adjust the blanket around Rachel. He caught a glimpse of her in the rear-mirror. The expressive face had disappeared with the make up, her eyes looked far away and unfocussed. He wondered whether she would feel angry at having to go. Beside him Rachel was shivering occasionally underneath her blanket.

On arrival at the cottage he stoked up the fire he'd lit earlier and helped Rachel bathe in the tiny bathroom. The hot water began to restore her and together they started counting the bruises.

"You're covered in them."

"I know," she said, inspecting the underside of her forearm. "I'm going to be black and blue." She drew her lips in in a resigned smile.

"So, what happened?"

Rachel stared at the soap trails in the water. She spun one around her finger. "I was climbing. That's right. I'd climbed onto the dry stone wall. You could walk along it. I was thinking; this is good. Then I was thinking... " she stopped: her finger stopped. "I was thinking about Kate, then the wall collapsed."

"What about Kate?"

Rachel continued to spin the soap into swirling Catherine-wheels. "I can't remember." She looked up at him. Her thick hair, now damp, was brushed back. Richard felt he could recognize every freckle on her face; he leant down and kissed her eyelids.

Rachel fixed him with a serious stare. "What were you and Kate doing outside last night?"

"Nothing."

"What were you laughing at?"

"I told you. A joke."

"I saw you from the window."

Richard stared down at the dirty bath water. "Saw what?"

"Together." Rachel put a soapy hand on his arm. "Richard please be honest with me. I've tried so hard to make things work."

As if the alcohol had merely postponed it, for the first time since the previous night, he felt totally humiliated. "We were drunk, just fooling around."

"Do you fancy Kate?"

"No." Richard felt the same sense of dread he'd felt, when as a child he'd attempted to lie to his all-knowing mother.

"Who started it?"

"Both of us." It didn't sound very convincing. "It just happened."

"I think you'd better ask Kate to leave."

"Yes."

Rachel squeezed his arm. "Now."

There was no one in the kitchen when Richard poked his head round the door. He checked Kate's bedroom but there was no reply. Puzzled, he went back downstairs. Her bags were by the door. Hearing the clunk of a car door he went outside and bumped into Kate, walking back towards the cottage.

"You're not going are you." Richard's voice sounded too relieved for it for it to be a question.

Kate stopped. She looked at him scornfully. "You don't think I'd give you the pleasure of asking me to go, do you?" Pushing past him she went inside and stood by her bags, her arms folded.

"Let me take those."

Kate snorted. The toe of one of her shoes tapped angrily on the concrete.

"I think Rachel wants to spend a bit of time on her own. She's a bit shaken up."

Kate looked at him incredulously. "I'm not bloody surprised. Are you always so bloody insensitive?"

Richard spoke over his shoulder as he carried the bags outside. "I'm sorry it had to be like this."

Kate swarmed past him and a finger-nail stung his chest. "And what makes you think it bloody well had to be like this?" She stood in front of him, her hands on her hips. "You ungrateful little gob-shite. I don't know what story you told Rachel. But I do know one thing. It won't have been the bloody truth!" She raised her voice and a finger-nail slashed the air in front of Richard's face. "You should be bloody grateful to me that I'm going." Turning on her heel she marched off to the car.

Richard followed her and stacked the bags into the boot. Closing it he found he didn't know what to do with his hands and ran a finger foolishly along the trim on the back door. When he reached the end, caught in Kate's stare, he was incapable of taking it off. "Look, about last night, I'm sorry."

Kate sneered at him. "Yeah, so am I."

Richard wiped a black smear from off the end of his finger as Kate started the engine and wound down the window.

"Give me love to Rachel. Tell her I'll be in touch, and tell her I understand." The car pulled away down the drive.

Richard's eyes followed it as it swung out into the road, dipped and then headed along the edge of Derwent Water. He stared after it for some time until it had vanished completely. Then, turning, he looked thoughtfully up at the ridge behind the cottage where the waterfall was clearly visible, leaping and tumbling its way down into the valley, sighed, wiped a black smear off the end of his finger, and went back in to Rachel.

Alan Wilkinson

REMEMBER THE ALAMO

So today I get to the office real early to start on another piece about the crime rate, and whaddayou know, there on my desk's this morning's "Journal" with a front page story all highlighted in luminous yellow. A homicide, the fiftieth of the year already, and I'm saying to myself shit, things are going from bad to worse in this town, and that's about as far as I get because no sooner do I sit down than my editor's on the phone.

He wants five hundred words by eleven o'clock. Something different this time. No more of that anti-gun lobby crap, he says. Let's have something about the human psyche. Why do people shoot each other over a ball game, for chrissake? Give us a bit of psychology. That's your thing, ain't it? he says. Didn't you write a book about that one time?

Yeah, it's my thing, I guess. I did major in psychology, way back. And peace studies. And Ban The Bomb. Make Love not War. Kill The Pigs – no, scrub that. I was never into that. I've always detested violence. Written two books and God knows how many articles and editorials about it.

So I sit down and try it, brainstorming, the way I always do. But it won't come, and pretty soon I go get myself a cup of coffee and start again. But nothing. So I pick up the paper and cut out the story – Man Killed in Central Ave. Bar Shoot-Out – and read it, and you know what I do? I –

No, let me just think a minute before I start on this, although why I should go in for a lot of denials and maneuvrings and shifting positions to dodge a whole bunch of imagined flak I don't know. These editorials don't even carry a by-line.

Who's to say if it's contrived or not?

Who's gonna care, for chrissake?

The fact of the matter is – and here I find myself coughing, or rubbing the side of my nose, or uncrossing my legs, or wishing I could hide behind a false accent... in any case crucify style... fact is, when I read it through and it's in the old Alamo of all places and they were fighting over the World Series I can't help a little grin and a whoop as I take it down the corridor tagged to my clip-board with all my morning's scratched-out notes, flapping there, a half-column report full of eye-witness accounts, names and addresses, and a car chase up Central.

I burst into Joe's office and show it to him. "Hey," I say, "remember the Alamo?" but the guy's busy talking on two phones at once and I figure it'll wait, so I wander back to my desk thinking about it.

*　　　　　*　　　　　*

I was in grad school, and we used to drink in this little dive right across from the campus on old Route 66 where they served big spilly pitchers of yellow piss-beer, except mostly you drank straight form the bottles to prove how tough you

were – Dos Equis, Herman Joseph, Tecate – and watched the
ball game. Always a ball game on T.V. Two World Series and
two Superbowls I sat through, and I remember that first year
wondering why all the cheering for Boston and their big-deal
hero – I forgot his name now – two thousand miles away back
east, but having the good sense to keep my mouth shut for
once until I realised they were playing the Yankees and it was
okay to root for any side that might cream those mothers.

Dark in there, the way bars are dark out west. Just the place
for secretly getting a little high, lunchtime, watching for the
glare of light every time the door swung open, thirsty enough
for that first bottle or two to tip your head and swallow swallow
swallow until your eyes watered and the fizz in your throat
hissed up and made your head float for just a second and made
you feel really fucking heroic.

Like the time I was on my own and that gorilla came, tower-
ing over me, four feet wide and ham hands swathed in filthy
bandages, tattooed shoulders, and leans right over me, except
I never really saw the size of him at first, just the creased sag
of his jeans bellow his belly, and I heard his voice. "D'you
believe in Gawd A'mighty and Jeez Christ our Lawd an'
Saviour?" and I never gave it a thought, just laughed a little
snort of beer down my nose and said, "Are you serious?"
thinking maybe I was in some quiet little scene in someone's
back yard amongst friends at a table full of ho ho college
liberals, not alone and dreaming between a morning's grass
cutting out in the steel heat and an afternoon's Western Lit.
in that air-conditioned windowless room over the road there,
Humanities 216.

Soon as it was out I thought, what the fuck have I said now?
He had a knife in his belt about eight inches long and a black
strap around his wrist all studded to hell, and he grabbed my
shoulders and leaned over real close and showed me his red
shot eyes, tombstone teeth and split lips. "'Cos I don' like no

motherfuckin' heathens, boy," and I kept on staring at the T.V. much as I could through his armpit. I remember the drip of sweat there, hanging like snot from an old man's nostril.

Yeah, maybe I do owe my life or something to the man at the strike, whoever he was. I watched him spit, lean back real easy and slug one way over centre field, up up up hovering there above the rows and rows of upturned faces. "'Cos one thing I can't stand is them atheistic sonsabitches. S'what's wrong with this goddam country, right boy?" And as the ball landed in the top tier and all the hands went up for it like it was one of those prayer revivals the place just about erupted and the guy let go of me to see what was happening and held up his fists in triumph before going to the bar to collect on a bet he'd made with a crowd of bikers there.

While the hero of the day was loping from first base to second to third, grinning up at the basin of screaming fans and then wheeling away to get jumped on by all the boys from out the bull pen, and the trainers and the manager and the owner and every mother's son of them, and my Biker for Christ was passing his scrunched up winnings over the bar for another pitcher, I drank up and walked out of there.

I cut across Central, over the grass in the shade of the tall trees and did a spot of shaking, and spat a few times. Soon as I got over to the Humanities I went to the men's room, stripped off, and washed my hands and arms and shoulders and brushed my hair and then went and looked around the department for someone to talk to until three o'clock when my class started.

I ran into Joe. I said, "Hey, I thought you'd left town. Haven't seen you in two three weeks," and he told me he'd been out of action since he got mugged and beaten, right outside his home up in Wyoming. He'd just cashed his pay-check and two guys jumped him and took off with three hundred bucks. "Shit," I said, and he said, "Yeah, they kicked the shit right outa me all right." And then he grinned at me, that grin you see on so many young guys these days in their late twenties or so – all mouth and beautiful straight teeth – and you have to look to their eyes to read the message there, about what they've been through and what they sure as hell ain't gonna put up with no more. The look of a hero. Yeah. It's there in their cold eyes, and in the end it gets to where you hardly want to trust a guy who ain't got that look, because otherwise you figure you don't know shit. "Yeah," he said, still grinning real tight, "but that's the last time this guy gets mugged. I went out and bought me a gun, man."

So then I told him about my crazy biker and he laughed, for real this time, and said, "Shit, don't you just meet the wackiest characters down at the Alamo?"

But later, when we were having coffee together after class, I told him. I said, Jesus, I could kill bastards like that. No kidding. Not with my hands, I said – hey, take a look at me: five feet six and a hundred and thirty pounds – no, but put a gun in my hand and I'd do it. Yeah, cool and patient, outside across the street, say. Waiting in the shadows. And when he comes out, blinking in the light – pop. Like that.

Joe looked at me real surprised. Said he always thought I was Mr. Nice Guy, and I said yeah, sure I am. It's easy, ain't it? You go round being nice in your space, and all you want is for everybody else to do the same, in their space. Then some day you get cornered... right?

Funny how things stick in your mind. That was the year peace finally broke out, and we all put away our buttons and bumper stickers, and got into the environment and all of that. Then Joe and I graduated and got jobs with the same paper.

*   *   *

So I pick up the clipping and try Joe's office again. He's sitting drinking a diet Coke. "Hi, how ya doin'?" he says.

"Can't seem to get into it this morning," I tell him, and then I pass the clipping across and he glances at it and grins at me and says yeah, he already saw it. "Man," he laughs, "we had us some good times there, didn't we? Cowboy country. I guess the old frontier spirit lives on down there, eh? A guy starts rooting for the wrong team and you pull a gun and" – he aims two fingers at me, squinting over the top of his fist – "pop." And he blows the smoke away, just like in the movies. He laughs again, remembering with affection. "Yeah, the old Alamo. Man!" Then he stretches back in his swivel chair and rubs his stomach. "How do I look? I've lost twenty pounds already." I tell him he's looking real good. "So, what's new?" he asks.

"Oh... " I shrug my shoulders. "The crime rate's going up, is all." And I look at my notes and check my watch. Ten fifteen already. "So, what can I say about violence in forty-five minutes, Joe?"

Biographies

GERRI BRIGHTWELL I am twenty-three, have had over twenty jobs, worked in France, Spain, Israel, the USA and Greece, lived on a barge, started a degree in zoology and finished a BA in Humanities, and am now writing in Norwich.

BARBARA COCKS was born in New Zealand in 1949, the daughter of a well-known watch-maker. She studied English Literature at the University of New South Wales, French poetry at the Universite Libre de Bruxelles and Latin American Literature at the University of Cambridge where she obtained her doctorate in 1983. After the downfall of Whitlam, she left Australia, and began a series of wanderings during which she lived in Asia, Latin America, Europe and Scandanavia. She is best known for her theatre reviews in Tharuka, her letters to the Bulletin, and her contributions to the now defunct Nation Review. To obtain a visa for her residence in Brussels she married a well-known Polish house renovator and scientist who now cares for her two children. Barbara Cocks is currently working on the draft of a novel.

SUZANNAH DUNN was born in 1963. A novella with short stories (including *Mother Love*) will be published by Serpent's Tail in 1990.

CAROLINE FORBES I am 37, white, originally from London though now living permanently in Norfolk. As a lesbian feminist I see my writing as a way of explaining my politics, celebrating and evaluating the lesbian community I live in and challenging assumptions of 'normality' in today's society. I have worked variously as a teacher, care assistant, postwoman, museum curator and, at present, computer trainer. I have had a collection of lesbian feminist science fiction short stories published – *The Needle on Full* (Onlywomen Press 1984)

ANDREW GARVIN Born in Leeds 9.6.50, educated local primary, grammar school. Left latter at fifteen to study at FE college. Corresponded with Herr de Vries of Bureau de Recherches Surrealistes, published poétry in Brumes Blondes, (Amsterdam). Studied French, History, English at Portsmouth Polytechnic; wrote study of Valery's Cahiers at Orleans; PGCE at Keele. Wrote an enormous quantity of letters in French and English. Taught in England and France; moved to Armagnac to live in a deserted abbatoir. Organiser of Wood Green CND and Multicultural Peace Festival. Moved to Greece, married, began writing a novel in progress, *Happiness in Ithaki*.

ROLF HUGHES was born in 1963. He has written and performed material for the theatre and played guitar in a number of modern jazz groups. His previous work has been broadcast on BBC radio and published in an anthology of verse and prose – *Hard Lines 3* (Faber and Faber)

SAUL HYMAN was born in London in 1958. After attending Bedales School and Trinity College, Cambridge he taught English in Zimbabwe for two and a half years. He has worked for the British Council and BBC Enterprises and is currently writing a novel based on his experiences in Zimbabwe.

DENISE NEUHAUS Born in Suffolk and brought up in Texas, has lived in London for the past five years. She has worked as a waitress, secretary, potter's apprentice, domestic, bartender, cook, banker, journalist and management consultant. She is currently working on a novel.

MARK SLATER Born 1956. Educated at Woolverstone Hall School. Degree in Literature and Philosophy at Sussex University. Has worked as a professional musician, furniture designer and college lecturer. Teaches creative writing in East Sussex. Is currently working on a libretto and a collection of short stories.

ALAN WILKINSON has worked as a rat-catcher, freight train guard and immigration officer. At the age of thirty-five he took a degree in American studies at the University of Hull. He is now broke.